In The Garden

Catherine Ritch Guess

CRM BOOKS

CRM, P.O. Box 367
Paw Creek, NC 28130
www.ciridmus.com

Publisher's Cataloging-in-Publication
(*Provided by Quality Books, Inc.*)

Guess, Catherine Ritch.
    In the garden / Catherine Ritch Guess. --1st ed.
    p. cm.
    LCCN 2002090518
    ISBN: 0-9713534-1-7

    1. Children of cancer patients--Fiction. 2. Cancer--
Patients--Fiction. 3. Mother's Day--Fiction.
4. Hendersonville (N.C.)--Fiction. 5. Christian
fiction. 6. Domestic fiction. I. Title

PS3557.U34385I68 2002   813'.6
                    QBI02-701348

Acknowledgments

To Mildred Spencer, my aunt, for years of wonderful and humorous family anecdotes

To Betty Guess, my mother-in-law, for crafting the book title and my name in cross-stitch to match the cover

To Bonnie Johnson, for providing the spark that became my opening chapter, and for lending her years of professional medical knowledge and experience

To the nurses and staff of Margaret R. Pardee Memorial Hospital, Hendersonville, NC

Dr. Douglas B. Huntley, Dr. Stuart Glassman, Dr. Charles A. Albers and the staff of Carolina Surgeons, Hendersonville, NC

Dr. William D. Medina and the staff of Hendersonville Hematology and Oncology, Hendersonville, NC

To Dr. Russell Shoemaker and the nurses at Pardee Urgent Care, Hendersonville, NC

To Harriett Coffey, a Charlotte, NC, radio personality, and a five-year cancer survivor whose positive outlook has ministered to many who have listened to her show, and whose energetic spirit served as an inspiration for me during my mother's surgery and the trips up and down the mountain

To Fred Trachsel, a beloved teacher to all who know him, First Baptist Church, Hendersonville, NC

To the staff at Union Regional Medical Center, Monroe, NC, who graciously helped in my research of the events surrounding my birth at their hospital

And to all the mothers and daughters who have travelled the path of Cheree and Rosemary

About the Cover

A very special word of thanks goes to Plaid Enterprises, Inc. for permission to use the Bucilla Cross-Stitch design #64182 on the cover.

The original wording in the design reads, "One is nearer to God's heart in a garden than anywhere else on earth."

The Story Behind the Cover

My husband's maternal grandmother, Bertha Watts, was like many women of her generation who had to have some type of needlework in their hands at all times. The cross-stitch design by Bucilla, which is featured on the cover, was the last piece she started. Her final two years were spent in a healthcare facility, where she still tried to use her hands whenever possible. However, as time went by, that became more and more impossible for her.

After her death, this piece of started cross-stitch was among the things found in her room. Her only daughter, my mother-in-law, took the piece and finished it as a lasting tribute of her mother for herself and her four brothers.

One evening while visiting my mother-in-law for dinner, I happened to catch a glimpse of the cross-stitched pillow on the bed of the guest bedroom. For whatever reason, which I'm sure was an act of God, the pillow demanded my attention. I grabbed it, and took it into the dining room and proclaimed that I wanted that design for the cover of my Mother's Day book.

The first thing I did was to contact Bucilla. Lauren Powell, of Plaid Enterprises, Inc., called me back with permission to use the design on the cover. I was elated.

Next, I called Jerry DeCeglio, the graphics designer for my book covers. He was not sure my idea would work, but I had no doubts. Between knowing where my idea had come from, and knowing Jerry's ability to make all my ideas actually work on paper, I was most confident that I would see a cross-stitch pattern on my book cover.

Jerry scanned the pillow, using his creative tricks-of-the-trade, while I anxiously watched. What came out was a perfect picture of what I wanted on the cover. I'll never forget that morning. Jerry looked at the scanned copy in excited amazement, and kept saying, "This is great! This is great!"

I smiled, and humbly corrected, "This is God," to which we both nodded in agreement.

The next obstacle was to match the fabric and thread after

several years, so that the book title and name could be cross-stitched to match the design. I knew my mother-in-law could handle that area. I chose the fabric and thread from her craft drawer, and she called me the next day with the two items I needed.

Jerry was able to scan all three pieces of cross-stitch in layers to give me exactly what I wanted, then added the stripes I envisioned in my head to finish off the cover. He even made the back cover an added touch for me.

So, between several creative and imaginative minds, guided by One Source, we came up with a perfect marriage of a book and its cover.

You know the old saying, "You can't judge a book by its cover." In the literary world, that is completely untrue. Many people DO judge a book by its cover. My mission from the outset has been to have beautiful covers that act as a prelude to the content of my books. And thanks to Bucilla and Plaid Enterprises, Inc., that is DEFINITELY true in this case.

One is nearer
God's heart
in a garden
than
anywhere else
on earth.

To my mother,
Corene Ritch,

who used only
one
Guidebook
in raising her child

Happy Mother's Day,
May 12, 2002

Foreword

They say that the best fiction is based on true experiences. If that is the case, this book should be a winner. For I was born on Mother's Day, 1954, and in 2001, I was spending my birthday and Mother's Day with my mother, who was battling the cancer that we had just learned was in her body.

In my despair of finding a gift that would truly convey the depth of my love and appreciation for her, I happened to walk in the grocery store. All of the magazines and tabloids, mostly empty words, caught my eye.

The rest is history — or rather, In the Garden — for I rushed to my laptop and poured out this novella, named for my mother's favorite hymn, during the next two weeks that I spent with her. Most of the events are true stories, many unembellished, that portray a mother's love for her child, and the desire to give that child a perfect life.

On that count, my mother achieved her goal. No one could have had a happier childhood than I did. I was not given the world. But I was given what I needed — not so much materially - but mentally, spiritually and emotionally. I was taught that any dream had to be planted, watered, and reaped, but most importantly, nurtured. No talent, no matter how God-given, came without much practice.

To that end, I owe everything I have or own to my mother . . .

I love you, Mama - -

CR?

Proceeds from the sale
of this book
will go to
the new cancer wing
of
Union Regional
Medical Center

Monroe, NC

*In the
Garden*

One

I sat on the spacious screened porch looking out over the garden. The garden was full of life, yet provided a perfect spot of isolation to sit and relax while I thought back over the many volumes of memories that revolved around my mother. Memories that were accented by the picturesque scene in front of me, wherein lay a beauty that spoke of many phases of her life.

For in the garden were rows of rose bushes, of varied types and colors, that had been planted by the artist who lived here before my parents. They were the pride and joy of his wife, an invalid, who could see them from her bedroom window. There were patches of irises, phlox and daylilies that had once splattered the yard of my maternal grandmother with color. And there were rows of zinnias, callas, and dahlias that had once bordered the sides of my paternal grandmother's yard, separating it from the vast fields of crops and the farm that provided their sole supply of food. Lastly were my favorites - the familiar hyacinths, hollyhocks, and buttercups that had made the move from the house where I had been raised.

The pile of mail that had accumulated during the course of the past several days was much heavier than normal. And the routine assortment of bills did not look any more inviting than usual, so I opted to weed through all the cards and letters. As I thumbed through the bulky stack of envelopes, trying to decipher the birthday cards from the Mother's Day cards and the thinking-of-you notes, a church newsletter fell into my lap from the stack, begging to be read. My eyes skimmed over its pages, stopping when a small italicized blurb caught my attention.

If I had a flower for each time I thought of my Mother, I could walk in my garden forever. - author unknown

My first reaction to that quote was a dampening of my eyes. But as I read over the words several more times, delving deeper into my consciousness with each reading, a garden unfolded in my mind. I closed my eyes and began to envision a flower for each memory of my mother.

A garden indeed!

The quote in itself was a touching sentiment, but what struck me most profoundly was the fact that many of the fond memories of my own mother were born in a garden - or at least *stemmed* from a garden. I laughed at my own ingenuousness. *No pun intended*, I grinned, *but I'll take it for what it's worth! Humor may be a bit hard to come by over the next few days.*

I read the quote again, this time finding the words "author unknown" most intriguing. The author had, in reality, been the mother of the speaker, not the person who had first uttered the words. *A flower for each memory.*

Captured in a melancholic daze, I glanced around the garden at the flowers that were springing up from the earth all around the bench. As beautiful as the varied colors of the blooms were, there were not nearly as many flowers as the number of memories that I had of my mother.

Usually, the morning air was very still here, holding in the brisk chill of the cool mornings, but this morning there was just enough of a gentle breeze to fan the white lace curtains peeking out from behind the slightly opened window.

How much that sight reminded me of my mother's presence. Such a small, petite woman, extremely soft-spoken, if she even spoke at all. Yet when she did speak, what she said was filled with spirit, a spirit

3

akin to the gentle breeze of the morning - a wind strong enough to move the curtains, but gentle enough that it seemed they moved of their own free will. *Exactly the same phenomenon as her ability to persuade her daughter to make the right decisions.* A gentle suggestion that you noticed was there, but that did not move you against your will.

I eyed the curtains again, knowing they were calling me back into the house to check on my mother who was lying just beyond them.

I watched as my father used the merry-tiller to turn the earth so that he could plant the green beans and tomatoes that Mama loved so much. After he finished a small patch, he moved to a spot slightly removed from their bedroom window so that he could plant some flowers where she could see them when she was sitting up in the bed.

Does he understand how difficult this is for Mama? Is he in denial, or can his own life's experiences even allow him to understand the depth of the seriousness here?

The seriousness? . . . Seriousness.

Serious, a word that rewound my mental recall mechanism as the same word that gently escaped from my father's lips on that Friday - the day that my fears were confirmed by the doctor, and that Mama's battle for life began.

Daddy sat in the waiting room talking to Jim and me, rattling off tales from his childhood. The stories were like familiar fairy tales to me, but they were a way of entertaining Jim, *or Daddy!*, as I now looked back at the situation. He gave his son-in-law an insight into his own past and opened an opportunity for a bonding and a trust that would serve to be most beneficial between them in the coming days and weeks.

Just how soon that trust would begin was unknown to me until the next sentence escaped my father's lips.

"I just don't know what I will do if this is anything serious."

My heart stopped as I glanced over at Jim, who was staring back at me with the same look of trepidation. At that instant it hit me like a bomb that had left its recipients in shellshock, as I realized that Daddy had no clue as to what was going on back in the surgical suite.

What I did know was that the doctor was going to come through the door, facing us at any minute with the details of my mother, and my father was going to be devastated. I looked into his eyes, eyes that had given me comfort for nearly five decades, knowing that the time had come for me to reciprocate.

"You'll just do what you have to do, Daddy. You know God always gives us what we need."

I did not have time to prepare a more convincing statement, or offer more encouragement, for at that moment the huge metal doors swung open and Dr. Atkins walked toward us, carrying several sheets of pictures.

The surgeon moved the newspapers from the corner chair and took a seat, so as to be in the center of his audience when he shared the results of the tests with us. His slight pause before he began to speak told me everything I needed to know. I rose from my seat so that I could hold onto Daddy when he heard the news.

Bracing myself for the worst, I heard the words cut through the room like a machete, slicing open everything that stood in their way. "I'm terribly sorry, but there's just no easy way to put this." I heard a quick gasp from my father as the doctor continued, "Mrs. Miller has a malignancy, a very large malignancy, that has apparently been in her rectum for quite some time."

The fact that my heart had ceased beating only moments earlier did not matter, for Daddy's heart began to pound so hard and fast that it made up for both of us. In fact, I was afraid his heart was literally going to jump right out of his chest. I held my hand fast to his back, trying to massage it gently, yet firmly enough to relieve any of the stress that had just taken over his body. Although I knew the initial shock would allow him to keep going for a while, I realized that this was the hardest thing my dad would ever have to deal with - the hardest thing, almost. There was only one thing that would ever be any tougher on him. Immediately, my prayers expanded from not only protecting and healing my mother, but to guarding and strengthening my father to

6

be able to deal with the worst ordeal of his life.

Here were my parents, only a little over a year away from their golden anniversary, when devastation took hold of their lives. My parents had grown in the awe-revering way that a couple does after that many years together. In them, I could see the ultimate reward of marriage that divorce had robbed from society, that ability to learn and accept and appreciate all the bad and the good, including all the differences in personality types that begin to cause so much dissension once the honey-moon is over.

It struck me that even in their differences, my parents had truly become best friends. They shopped together, they read together, they ate together, they had literally become inseparable. The one thing that I had grown to admire so greatly about my parents all of a sudden seemed like their very doom.

My dad's comment from minutes earlier rang through my head again. No, he didn't know what he would do if this turned out to be something serious. Now it was serious, but he at least still had his mate. What *was* he going to do if he lost her? Now *I* didn't know what he would do if it became that serious.

Why all of these thoughts were flying through my head at the moment was beyond me, but I had the good sense still left to ignore my own thoughts and fo-cus solely on Daddy, for Mama had a wonderful doctor and the Great Physician taking care of her.

Okay, Rosemary. There you go. Just follow the same

advice you gave a few minutes ago, and you will have every-thing you need to get you, AND DADDY, through this - no matter what the outcome.

The surgeon's words had still been ravaging their way through my head, even with my thoughts trying to take over, to the point that I had heard every single one.

"The mass is like a huge donut that has man-aged to surround her entire abdominal wall, and has grown to the point that it has stretched and pulled on her internal organs until the walls have ripped. That is where all the blood is coming from."

"All the blood"? Okay, it is time for a confessional here. Someone has been leaving me out, keeping me in the dark, and I do not like it.

I knew that I could not hound Daddy right now, but as soon as the dust settled, someone was going to have to clue me in to what had been going on with my mother recently. This situation had just escalated to be-ing much worse than they had admitted to me. And since my mother was apparently in no condition to give me the information, my father was my only hope. *If she even confided in him.*

I knew Mama was of the generation who was very private with their lives - mentally, emotionally, and physically - but I knew that was all going to have to change, and in a major hurry. The time of getting to the root, and I meant *root*, of the problem was at hand.

The surgeon did not give me time to figure out how I was going to get the necessary information for he began asking pertinent questions. Not firing them at Daddy, but asking them in an easy manner, trying to build a calm rapport with my father.

"When did the bleeding first begin?"

My ears perked up, and all thoughts became merely fleeting as I turned all my attention to this surgeon who had just moved up several notches in my book.

"I don't really know."

Bingo! I was right. Mama didn't tell him anymore than was absolutely necessary.

But I didn't let my mind wander. I turned immediately back to the question-and-answer session lest I miss any clues myself.

I heard Daddy continue, "She didn't tell me until about three weeks ago. We started trying to get an appointment with her regular doctor, but he could not see her for two months. We tried for another week to get an appointment with any doctor, but they either were not taking new patients, or had a long wait for appointments."

My father was doing a great job of relaying the information to Dr. Atkins. He did not even stop for a breather, or to get past an emotional break-down, as he gave the doctor all he could.

But why should he show emotion right now? He truly is in shock. Poor Daddy had absolutely no idea how bad things were, and this news surely had not begun to sink in yet, especially with him having to divert his full attention to helping the doctor right now.

9

Daddy kept rolling off facts in a steady, even pace, not rushed or panicked, but very matter-of-factly. "Finally, this past Tuesday, I told her, 'that was it,' after she stayed in the bathroom all night. 'That we were going to the Urgent Care facility.' Looking back, I guess she must have felt pretty bad because she finally agreed."

He was right. Cheree Miller had white-coat syndrome as bad as anyone I had ever seen, and I knew that for her to agree to go to a doctor, much less an emergency facility, was only one step lower than an act of God. It struck me that she also knew that, or she would not have consented even then. So in that strain of thought, my mother's decision truly *was* an act of God.

"When she saw the doctor at the Urgent Care, he said she needed to go straight to a surgeon. Since one of your associates took care of my melanoma surgery right after we moved here, we had them call his office. Your receptionist scheduled an appointment for the next day, and when Cheree saw Dr. Stallings this past Wednesday, he scheduled her for out-patient exploratory surgery today. He recommended you as the best guy for this particular job, but stated that you were unavailable until next week, and informed us that this should be handled immediately."

I hoped that my father did not catch the disdain in my eyes when I realized that even after the rush from one doctor to another and then to surgery, with an unscheduled doctor, he still had no idea as to the seriousness of my mother's condition. It was not a feeling toward him, but a hurt for him that he did not pick up on clues surrounding the situation.

But why should he? I asked myself, knowing he had no reason to have prior knowledge of how the medical world had become. Here were he and my mother, both whom had never gone to a doctor unless it was the last resort, hailing the symptoms a dire emergency. They did not know that even for an ingrown toenail, there was now a long wait and repeated visits. So this swift chain of events seemed normal to them from their own prior experience.

The sorrow for my dad, with his earlier statement about not knowing what to do "if this was anything serious" really tore at me. He was not ready for the shock of his life. The thought of my mother being in real danger never entered his mind. And now, as he talked to the doctor, the reality was still floating in the air somewhere above him, waiting for its own center stage.

I also saw the sorrow in the doctor's eyes, for now he also knew that my father was totally unprepared for the message he had just delivered. He reached over and put a strengthening hand on my dad's upper arm, looked sympathetically into his eyes, and spoke in the most tender of tones, as if he were speaking to a child.

"Mr. Miller, your wife needs surgery immediately. But, she has lost a lot of blood. We are preparing to do a blood transfusion this afternoon just to build her up enough to face the surgery, which we can hopefully do on Monday."

Sensing the strength and wisdom of the experienced doctor, my father looked at him with utmost confidence. "Will you be doing the surgery?"

"This is quite involved, so my associates and I will all be in the surgery."

The expression on Daddy's face showed that was all he needed to hear. He, at this point, realized that his wife was in good hands - the best, in fact – and he was content that he had done his part in helping Dr. Atkins.

As the surgeon carefully eyed my father's face to make sure he was alright, I asked my own question.

"Does she know yet?"

"She already knew. You can always tell when you speak to a patient, and it was evident that Mrs. Miller not only knew, but was at total peace with this. She never even lost her smile."

"That's my mom!", I proclaimed, fighting to hold onto a smile that, for the first time, threatened to burst into a flood of tears. As I watched the surgeon stand to leave, I prayed that I had inherited Mama's ability to keep my smile for Daddy's sake once the doctor was gone.

"We'll be checking on her during the day. She'll be back in her room in about thirty minutes, and you can visit with her for a while until they get her ready for the blood transfusion."

Daddy stood and reached out his hand. "Thank you, Dr. Atkins."

A part of me wondered how many other people

had ever thanked this doctor for delivering the most earth-shattering news of their life. And then I reflected silently, *That's my Pop!*, knowing that herein lay his strength. He was, after all, a Southern gentleman befitting of his charming Southern belle.

Dr. Atkins made his way back to the surgical suite. Jim stood, as did I, and we followed Daddy for a couple of steps further toward the back of the family waiting room. He took his handkerchief from his back pocket and blew his nose as the tears slowly made their escape. I held onto his arm with one hand and massaged his back gently with the other, while I was afforded the privilege of being consoled by my own spouse's tender hands on my arm and back.

Daddy turned to face us, wiping the tears and putting away the handkerchief. "I don't know what I would have done if you had not been here with me today. I don't think I could have handled this by myself."

"Now, aren't you glad I came?" I asked with a lighter tone to my voice. "And you weren't even going to call me!"

He nodded at me, picking up on my effort to keep a brighter spirit. "Yes. I just wasn't prepared for anything like this."

"I know," I said, with all of us embracing in a group hug, causing me to fight away my own tears even harder.

Daddy looked at me with a stoic face, trying to muster his strength back. "Were you expecting something like this?" he asked, with that sixth sense that parents possess, knowing that my presence was not merely by accident.

I didn't want to sound too presumptuous, but after all, it was him who taught me not to lie. My eyes looked into his, still pushing back the drops of water whose force was getting stronger by the second.

"Yes, Daddy. That's why I insisted on being here today. I knew that if Mama only went to the doctor on Tuesday, and they sent her to a surgeon the next day, who sent her to the hospital two days later, they were not expecting a routine examination."

My father looked at Jim. "What about you?"

"I knew to trust Rosemary enough that if she was concerned, I had better be here, too. So that's why I called in today at work and decided to come with her. I could tell from the expression on her face that I needed to be here worse."

"Well, you were right, and we both *did* need you. Thank you for being here for her." Daddy looked at me, his hands wiping stray tears. "I just can't thank you both enough."

There he goes, being that Southern gentleman again!

And now I see where Rosemary gets it! Jim thought, seeing how much of both her parents' mannerisms she had actually acquired.

"Can I get you anything before you go up to Mama's room?" I knew the answer even before I asked the question, but I wanted to make sure Daddy was okay.

14

"No, I'm just anxious to see my beautiful wife right now."

Jim and I exchanged glances, both fighting back even more tears at his sweet, yet most sincere, comment. My own heart longed to someday receive that same degree of love and devotion that was evident in his speech and actions.

"We'll be right up. I'm going to grab a drink real quick."

"Take your time. I'm fine."

My ears told me that Daddy was fine, but my heart told me to get the soda, guzzle it down, and get to Mama's room before she did. There was no way I was going to let him face this alone. We were a family, and we would lick this together.

Jim took my hand in his and turned me toward him as we watched Daddy turn the corner and walk down the hallway. He pulled me to him and hugged me long and hard, as if he could pass his own strength through his arms to my body. I rested my head on his shoulders briefly, and then looked back up into his face. He could see that my own emotions had taken a back seat until I got my father past this initial hurdle. And we both knew that the hardest part was yet to come, when my parents faced each other.

"Why don't you step outside and get some fresh air? I'll bring the drink to you."

I nodded, welcoming the chance to be alone for a few minutes to clear my head, collect my thoughts, and ask God for all I would need for the upcoming days, but most especially for the next hour or so.

Though I usually loved sitting on a park bench beneath shady trees, this was not one of those times. My body paced up and down the steps and sidewalk, making a circle around the entire front of the hospital. I knew that my tears were finding another way to vent themselves, and that my body was ridding itself of lots of nervous energy, so that I could appear completely settled when Mama got back to her room.

A couple of sips on the drink made me realize how hungry I had become during the course of the surgery. It had been eight hours since we had stopped for breakfast, but the role of being the concerned daughter subsided my own needs until this moment.

"Why don't you let me get you something to eat?" Jim asked, sensing my hunger.

And probably his own, I suspected. He had been exactly what I needed at this time in my life. I thought back to the night he had asked me to marry him. We had both been mature adults, and had some experience of living alone before we tied the knot, so I had an idea of what would be the most valuable quality to me in a spouse.

Looking into Jim's eyes, the conversation came back to me, lulling me away from the moment at hand, like a soft lullaby.

"I will not ever ask much of you, and yes, I will marry you, *if* you can promise me only one thing in life,"

I had challenged him.

"What's that?"

"If there ever comes a time that something happens to my parents, you will have to be there for me." He sat there, giving me an odd stare, as if that was a part of the whole deal, which it was, but there was much more of an urgency to it from my standpoint. I tried to make him understand my feelings. "Jim, I am an only child. My parents have always given up for me, and I fully expect to give them the same courtesy someday. You know what an independent person I am, all but refusing to accept help from anyone, but if the day *should* ever come when my parents need me, I will go to them. And not only that, but if there is ever a serious problem, someone had better be ready to hold me up, because that is probably the one time I will lose it. All I'm asking for is a strong arm when that time comes."

In all the time we had been together, I had never seen the level of tenderness, or depth of understanding, in Jim's eyes that I saw on that evening. Until now.

He had known full well what today's outcome was going to be as well as I did. He had a full schedule at work today. He had plans to go out with his friends to see a baseball game after work this evening. And he had a large project going on at work the next week that needed his attention today before the weekend. But when I had come out of the shower this morning, I saw him dressed in casual clothes rather than his usual suit.

"Where are you going today?" I asked, wondering if today's meeting was to be held on the golf course.

"With you," he said nonchalantly, buttoning his last button.

"But, honey, you can't do that. You've got so much…"

Jim had walked over to me by this point and taken my hands. "Rosemary, you have no idea what is going to happen today, and the way I see it, there is only one place for me to be. Anyone can take my place in the meeting, and handle every item on the day's agenda."

He had remembered the promise that he silently pledged in our vows, even without me reminding him. The words written all over his face told me that I did not have to wait until some day far away to have the same kind of love and devotion that Daddy had for my mother. I had it now. Maybe not the same magnitude that came from years of living together, but the same strong foundation.

It was most heart-warming to see him now, looking at me with huge eyes that carried no expression, but said they were here for me – both now and for the duration. My physical needs became unimportant as I clasped his hands and kissed them.

"I would really prefer to get back to Mama's room right now. Once she and Daddy have faced each other, and the shockwaves have turned to ripples, I'll come back down here with you and grab a bite. Besides, there will be several phone calls to make, and I'd just as soon not make them from her room. I think the time alone will do them good." I glanced over at Jim, hoping I wasn't being too selfish. "Why don't you go ahead and eat? You must be starving."

"I'm fine. You want to be there for Cheree and Mark. I want to be there for you."

I smiled and nodded. "Thanks," was all I could manage.

We made our way back to Mama's room in silence, as I spent my time in conversation with the *real* Doctor, now glad that Daddy had been clueless as to what was going on all this time. He had been spared many sleepless nights of worry, which I now realized as a true blessing instead of a sorrow.

As I approached the corridor leading to Mama's room, the pre-op nurse left her duty to meet me.

"What did you find out?" she asked, looking more like a naïve young girl, with her braids from a recent cruise, than a nurse who saved lives.

I could tell from the look in her eyes that she already knew. "She has cancer."

The pained expression in the nurse's eyes was most touching. My runaway mind immediately started assessing the situation of the woman who had been the first to hear that nightmarish phrase come from my lips. *Here is a woman who is in this field because it is where she wants to be. And here is a woman who makes a difference in the lives of the patients with whom she works. And here is a woman who is making a daughter more comfortable because the child now knows her mother is going to be well cared for.* That brief moment filled me with many realizations – realizations that were going to be crucial to me in the days and months ahead.

"What are they going to do?" she asked, her eyes still offering sympathy.

"She has lost so much blood that they are going to have to do a transfusion. They're trying to get her ready for surgery on Monday."

The nurse looked at me with eyes that obviously wanted more, but did not dare ask for fear of intruding. There was such an ambiance in her concern that I did not mind sharing.

"It doesn't look good," I offered.

"I was afraid of that." Comfortable that I was not threatened by her questions, the nurse continued, "How long has she been bleeding?"

"I'm not really sure. But apparently for quite a while."

"When I saw how she was bleeding this morning, I knew that something had to be done immediately."

"I know. I heard you go down the hallway and call the doctor out of surgery. Even though I'm not a nurse, I knew that was not standard operating procedure, if you'll excuse the pun. When the technicians came and took my mother, telling us that Dr. Atkins would be doing the procedure, because Dr. Stallings was not finished with the patient scheduled before her, I figured there was an emergency situation."

"I didn't want to frighten you, but she could not have lost much more blood. At the rate things were going, well . . . I'm just grateful you got her in here before the weekend. She would not have made it until Monday."

My head lowered, unable to speak or hear anymore. I thought of the little silver casting of monkeys that Rich had bought in Spain, the ones that had previously made me laugh at their portrayal of "See no evil, hear no evil, speak no evil." At the moment, I felt exactly as if I were one of those monkeys.

Obviously the nurse recognized my sentiments - ones that were probably common for many of the patients she saw. She asked no more questions, and I offered no more answers. I was glad that I at least had the good graces to thank her for her concern, and noted the name on her badge so that I could write her a note later.

Mama's pleasant smile made me wonder if the

21

doctor actually had told her anything, or if she had been so sedated that she did not comprehend his words. After all, she was so unaccustomed to taking any type of medication that her minute size would make her most susceptible. Her expression was totally undaunted as her bed was wheeled into the room.

Then it dawned on me. Her motherly strength was at work, refusing to show any weakness for her family's sake. The nurse went through the routine of making Mama comfortable, then excused herself so that we could get our reality checks in tow. No one mentioned the test, the upcoming surgery, nor the impending blood transfusion. Nothing. In fact, we were all standing there conversing as if there was nothing out of the ordinary going on at all, and Mama had just awakened from a nap.

When I saw that neither she nor Daddy were going to lose it, I took the initiative to move forward.

"Is there anyone you need me to call, or anything I can do for you, since it looks like you're going to be here a few days?"

Before Mama had time to pooh-pooh that idea, Daddy jumped in boldly, indicating that he would like for me to call a friend, who would then pass the word along through their church's prayer chain, and to the pastor, who was leaving to take another position during the course of the weekend.

"Then you might want to call Louise."

"No, you don't need to call her," I heard Mama

object.

I looked at the two of them, not wanting to create an argument, but not wanting to leave it up to them to settle this. "Mama, if *she* were having surgery, wouldn't *you* want to know?"

Oh, dear. I had crossed the boundary and said a bad word!

No one spoke.

Refusing to let silence take over, I defended my statement. "You know how much Aunt Louise is like Grandma Rose, and if someone doesn't call her, she's going to be madder than a wet settin' hen!" I injected, borrowing one of Grandma's frequent phrases, complete with her country rhetoric.

Still no one spoke. There was no anger or bitterness in the silence. It held only the courtesy from each of them, waiting for the other to give a seal of approval.

Another wonderful trait of a long and lasting marriage, I noted.

Finally it was Daddy who broke the silence. "Go ahead and call Louise. She has a right to know."

I glanced over at Mama. She didn't say a word, and the pleasant expression on her face never changed. *She also knows that I am going to call anyway*, I thought, aware that she did not see me as being disrespectful, only the headstrong Taurus that she had borne into the world. Besides, I knew that if she had really objected, she would have been more forceful, and both Daddy and I would have known to keep quiet.

A smug smirk made its way across my face. *Of course she could be thinking how she wished she had never been in the hospital forty-seven years ago!* I put my arm around her shoulder, hugging Mama's pillow more than her so as not to hurt her.

As if on cue, the nurse brought in a tray. I helped her push the cart across Mama's bed so that the food was right in front of the patient.

Picking up a towel and laying it across my arm, with the grace of a stylish waiter, I raised the silver cover from the tray, revealing its contents. "What delectable delicacies have we today?"

Mama laughed. "The doctor told me I could have a tray," she defended, knowing that I was questioning the fact of whether she could eat before the blood transfusion.

What I did not want to answer back to her was my hurt at looking at the offerings on the tray. The liquid beef bouillon, to be added to the hot water, the jello, and the juice said one thing to me. *Doom.* And I knew that my mother knew me well enough to catch the slightest emotion if I let my guard down. So the wall went back up.

"For an appetizer, we have Jellied Wild Cherry Souffle, for the entrée, we are featuring Beef Bouillon Wellington, to be followed by the finest of flamboyant, full-bodied and well-aged grape juice, south of California, 2001, and for dessert we have all-you-can-eat Saline Jubilee, better known as D5W."

Jim, my kitchen guru, looked at me in disbelief, amazed that I had managed to get it back together that quickly. I saw a wink dart my way, sealing his approval, both of my composure and my choice of menu items.

Daddy watched as I fed Mama the jello, saying how he wished he could do that. But we could hear in his voice that he really did not want to go there – not yet, while I was there to do it for him. He had never been a good nurse, and we all knew it just was not his cup of tea, so I dismissed him, trying to build his ego.

"I can do this. There are going to be plenty of other things you can do."

I wondered whether I had nudged them out of their comfort zone again. To be safe, I fed her in silence for the rest of her meal. As Mama finished the last swallow, I excused myself, sensing that the time had come for my parents to be alone.

x x x
x x x
x

Now comes the worst part!, I thought, dreading the job of calling Aunt Louise. She and my mom had already lost their only other sibling, a brother, to cancer, and I knew that she was going to be devastated. No one had even called to warn her of the impending announcement. Even though I had feared the worst, this was still worse than I had expected, and I felt it painfully unfair to have to call her from five-hundred miles away to break the news to her, having no idea if anyone was at home to console her. At least we had the doctor and each other on our end.

The dreaded call was no easier than I had anticipated. I heard the gasp and the tears that followed. And I felt terribly guilty for breaking the news to her in this manner. I apologized again and again, telling her that I wished there could have been another way, but that I knew she would want to know.

"Yes, you're right. I would have been madder than a wet settin' hen if you hadn't called me."

Okay, Daddy, what did I tell you? And even as badly as I felt for making the horrid call, I was gratified that I had taken the time to contact her.

There was a pause as I heard more tears. "I only wish I could be there. My reservations are for the 26th of this month, but maybe I can change my plane ticket."

"No, don't do that. We're all fine for the moment. There might come a time later that we need you worse than now. Why don't you wait and let's see what happens on Monday?"

"Well, okay. But if you need me, do you promise to call?"

"Yes, Aunt Louise, I do," I replied, remembering how she had stayed over once before on a visit, and sat with her brother through his final days.

Now I found myself praying that we didn't have

a recurrence of that episode, and I could tell, even through the receiver, that the same thought had just run through her head. More tears.

"Call me the minute you know something on Monday. I'll be sitting by the phone."

"I will. Just as soon as the doctors come out and give us a report, I'll call you while Mama's still in recovery. They said she'd be about an hour and a half." I could hear a door open in the background at Louise's house and the sound of young voices, which I recognized as her great-grandchildren. *Good! She's not there by herself anymore.*

"I'll be waiting. Tell Cheree and Mark that I love them, and I sure am sorry."

"Will do. And you take it easy. We've got everything under control on this end. Bye."

"Bye."

Tears gushed from the other end of the phone as I hung up. I knew that I had left my aunt, who had been like a second mom to me over the years, in a bad way. But I also knew that the best medicine for her at the moment was those two little girls that had just come through her door.

Thanks, God! Once again your timing is impeccable.

Standing there, still looking at the phone, my choice of words to my aunt struck me as being ironic. We had nothing in control. There was only One in charge of this situation. The only thing we were in charge of was our faith in that One, and the knowledge that that

27

same faith was going to be what carried us, individually and as a family, through this entire ordeal.

"Mom!"

The sound of a familiar voice cued my feet to pivot my body in the direction of it. My older son was bounding down the hallway with his usual, energetic basketball-player pace.

Yes, God, and was that bit about Your impeccable timing for Aunt Louise, or for me?

My son and I embraced, as I braced myself for one of the hardest things I would ever have to do. Doug, my firstborn son, was also the first grandchild on both sides of his family. He could have easily been a spoiled, rotten brat. But instead, he was full of love and respect for his elders, especially his grandparents.

And he had spent much of his infancy and childhood with his MaMa Cheree and PaPa Mark, since my private teaching studio had been connected to their house. All of his afternoons and evenings were spent with him worming his way into their hearts, and they into his. So, in all reality, they were more like his parents than his grandparents.

I knew that the news of Mama's cancer wa going to come as a crushing blow to him. My instincts took over my thoughts, as I saw God taking charge of this situation, also. I wrapped my arm in Doug's, and led him down the hallway to a family waiting room. While I fixed him a cup of coffee, I made small talk about his morning exam. There was no way I was going to break this news to him without being able to look him straight in the eye.

As I sat opposite him, I tried to find words to ease into the situation, but I was just as much at a loss as Dr. Atkins had been only a couple of hours before. Finally, the words simply poured out, as I felt them come from my mouth, in a motherly voice, which caressed them as they made their way across the room.

"Doug, the doctor found a large malignancy in your MaMa Cheree." I saw the lump form in his throat. The words kept shooting forward, lest I lose momentum while watching his reaction. "They are going to do surgery on Monday, but for now, she has lost a lot of blood, and they need to do a blood transfusion this afternoon." It was easy to see his mind trying to take in my words, and reprocess them, trying to decide whether they were real, or if he was in a bad dream. I felt the need for one last sentence, so as not to leave him in a total upheaval. "She's resting very comfortably in her room right now. Would you like to go and see her? Your PaPa Mark is there with her, too."

He nodded, setting the cup of coffee on the table. "Can I have a minute to go outside first, Mom?"

I knew the importance of that request. Doug, like his mother, needed a second to get his thoughts together, and being surrounded by God's nature at this beautiful time of year provided the perfect backdrop for that. I walked outside with him and sat quietly on the bench behind him. As he prayed his own prayer for his grandmother, I prayed for him in his own hurt.

When he turned to face me, I was relieved to see that there were no tears in his eyes. I stood, and we made the walk to Mama's room while I heard details of school and the exams of the last couple of days.

He's going to be alright, I thought as I listened to him. Pleasantly, I was reminded of how we come equipped for the things we need in life.

Jim, who had gone for a walk to give me a little privacy during my call to Aunt Louise, and to get my own thoughts together, saw us and came rushing down the hall in time to catch the elevator with us. He and Doug exchanged glances and nodded to each other, both realizing that was about as much as could be done without touching on the situation. Their understood silence made a statement to me of their mutual respect and concern - for each other, and for my mother.

We entered Mama's room and Doug walked over to her and gave her his usual hug accompanied by the words, "I love you, MaMa."

"I love you, too, Doug," she said, in the same bright-spirited, jovial voice she always used to speak to her grandsons.

The talk turned immediately to Doug's exams, and the gorgeous spring day. *Ah, weather*, I reminisced. *What would people talk about if it weren't for weather?*

To listen to the four of them, you wouldn't have known there was anything going on out of the ordinary. I felt most grateful that the only foreign object attached

to Mama at present was the IV tube. My better judgment told me that this "everything's normal" atmosphere
would not have been the same had their been all kinds
of tubes and machines hooked to her.

But for the moment, everyone was fine, and we
were all dealing with this horrendous invasion in our
own private ways, as well as a family.

A part of me wished to stay with them. A part of
me wondered what they would say to each other. A part
of me questioned whether they were able to say anything to each other.

Jim took my hand. "Relax, Rosemary. They're
fine. They've found a way to communicate for nearly
fifty years. I don't think they need you to start doing it
for them now."

His blunt frankness worked, for as well as forcing me see the truth in his statement, it also aroused a
smile. I was again reminded that I already *did* have someone who showered me with the same love and devotion
that my father had for my mother.

<pre>
x   x   x
 x x x
    x
</pre>

As we exited the hospital, knowing that I was going to be late for an evening appointment, I dialed the number of the florist whose work I had admired earlier in the day.

"Send my mother the most beautiful arrangement of flowers you can. I want a bright array of purples, pinks, blues and yellows. And find me some purple roses to mix in with the pinks." Jim looked at me as we walked shoulder to shoulder down the sidewalk. "No, that doesn't matter. I want it to be the most regal arrangement you've ever done."

My husband put his arm around me, not once scolding me for the fact that I had just told someone that it didn't matter the cost. But my next statement was unnecessary for his ears. It only served to justify my outrageous expense to myself . "I want to send her flowers while she can enjoy them."

He took my hand and squeezed firmly, as I walked down the rest of the sidewalk to the parking lot, head held high, proud of the senseless gift I had just bestowed on my mother. I was just as proud of the fact that I refused to allow myself to become depressed over the situation. The time for that would come tonight, after the rehearsal and dinner, when I could be alone to let my emotions run rampant.

There was only one goal in my mind now, and that was to get the incidental skirmishes out of the way so that I could give this battle the precedence it deserved. Having repercussions with myself that I was even leaving my mother's side to go home and take care of unfinished business, I reasoned that no good leader counteracts an attack without thinking through the scenarios and strategies.

I knew that I needed to sit down with my children and let them see that I was okay. My strength would be their cue as to how we were going to deal with this situation, and I intended to give them the same example of strength and faith that their grandmother had passed onto me. The manifestation of her legacy was fulfilling itself.

Then, of course there was the small matter of writing out job details for someone to take my place for the next few days, and getting my things together. There were some things that I had to get out of the way. Things that I knew could be handled by a substitute. But I knew people were counting on me, and my mother had taught me to be responsible and dependable. She would have felt bad had I not finished my business. And besides, this way it didn't appear that her family was sitting around giving in to this demon that had come into her path. Even though we were all in this together, I inwardly felt that she and Daddy both needed and deserved some time together.

And I also knew that Doug was the mightiest warrior that she could have taking care of her right now. There was no way that anyone was going to mistreat his grandmother, or that she would not get the best of care as long as he was there, and I was willing to bet that he would not leave the hospital until I got back on Sunday.

Somehow, looking at my calendar made the weekend's functions seem worse than I had imagined. *A wedding rehearsal, a rehearsal dinner, a wedding, and the youth choir concert and service, plus the extra rehearsals. Was I out of my mind?*

Even on an ordinary weekend, that schedule was enough to make one's head spin. *Nope, Rosemary Ellis, we will get through all of this.* The concentration of the required duties would keep my mind from having idle time to worry or think the worst, and it would help to build up my strength that I was going to need for the next while. And it would also put some closure on several areas so that I could take all the time I needed for my mother in the coming days and weeks.

Closing my planner, I felt a shudder run up my spine. It was not from the events of the day, but rather like a ghost of the past. Not even a shade of déjà vu, but something more intense, like seeing the image of someone from the grave. Whatever it was had materialized at the very instant I closed the datebook.

I opened the calendar again, slowly turning the pages to the right date. Nothing struck me as peculiar. My eyes examined the appointments carefully, looking for a clue as to why this sudden uneasiness had come over my whole being. Wracking my brain to figure out what was gnawing at me, I began to close the book once more.

A voice in the back of my head whispered, "I want to send her flowers while she can enjoy them."

It was the same phrase I had spoken to Jim earlier, but it was not my voice. What was causing this reaction? And furthermore, what did it have to do with the calendar?

I closed my eyes, and leaned back in the swivel office chair, letting the words filter through my mind, trying to catch not only the voice, but also the reason for their alarm. The words were so soft that I could could barely hear them, much less recognize the speaker. But as I played them in my mind over and over, it struck me that the voice was that of my own mother.

Okay. One down. Now what does this have to do with anything?

With my eyes still closed, I tried to picture my mother, and why she would be speaking those words to me. *I want to send her flowers while she can enjoy them. I want to send her flowers. I want to send her. Her, who? . . Her, who? . . . Her, who? . . . .*

I spoke the dates. Nothing rang a bell. *Perhaps you're barking up the wrong tree, Rosemary. You're probably just overreacting to a fearful situa . . .*

"I want to send her flowers while she can still enjoy them." It was my mother's voice, and she was calling me on the telephone on a Saturday morning. I had come home from college and was getting dressed to go play for a wedding, then rush back to school for a college choir concert. Trying to do too much at one time, I almost did not answer the telephone. But at the last minute, I decided it might be an important call.

"Rosemary," I could still hear her saying, "I'm glad I caught you. I know you're in a rush, but I need you to look up the number of the florist for me."

I had never been one to question my mother's authority, but she was not one to waste money on extravagancies, especially on the spur of the moment, much less when she knew that she was inconveniencing someone else. Given all the variables, I could not help it when I heard my voice unconsciously reply, "Why?"

"Your dad and I are at the hospital with your Aunt Peggy. She's just taken a turn for the worse. "I want to send her flowers while she can enjoy them."

Oh dear God! My mind raced through the five minutes that had followed that phone call. I had called the florist and ordered the flowers, just in time to catch my mother's next call, telling me to call the florist back and change the bouquet to a funeral basket.

Please, God, no. Please. . .

I could not even finish the prayer. My fingers quickly slammed the planner shut, as I shoved it back into the desk drawer, thrusting my mind into the activities of the weekend and away from the chill I had just had. The short span of the next three days had just become the longest seventy-two hours of my life.

Two

There was a message on the answering machine when I finally got home from the rehearsal. I pushed the play button out of habit, already beginning to unwind after the long emotion-wrenched day.

"Hi, Mom. I want to go and see MaMa Cheree. Can we go right after I get off work tomorrow afternoon and spend the evening with her, then come back on Sunday?"

I quickly ran 'reality' versus 'want' through my

head and knew there was no way to grant Rich's request. But I also knew that I was going to do as much as possibly laid within my control. My fingers quickly dialed the number of his dad's house, where he was staying for the weekend.

"Hello."

I spoke with the voice on the other end of the phone several times each day, but this time, it grabbed me by surprise. No longer was my little Rich my baby boy. He had grown into a strapping young man. This was not like a major reality, for I had noticed it gradually happening every time we went clothes shopping during the past few years. And I saw it each morning as I watched him leave for school. And I heard it in his voice every day when he sang with the radio. But there was something about the present urgency in his voice, not like the childlike pleas that I had heard when he was younger, but a persistence that rang with a maturity that had learned the richness of relationships over the years. It was the voice of a high school senior who had known an entire childhood of the love that only a grandmother could give to a young child.

The desire to grant my child's wish now became a necessity – a necessity borne out of the same urgency that I had just heard in his voice.

"Hi, Rich. I got your message."

"Good, can we go?"

All reason left me as my mind took in all the elements and devised a plan that would reach a compromise of everyone's schedules and still grant my son this wish.

"I have a wedding tomorrow at three. What time do you get off?"

"Three. How about if I drive across town as soon as I get off? That should give you just enough time to finish the Widor *Toccata* and get out the door."

A chuckle ran through my brain as I made a note that Rich had just selected the recessional for his own wedding ceremony for someday down the road. "Sounds like a plan to me. Now about spending the night, I have a special service with the youth on Sunday morning, so I will have to be back here. I don't think we can spend the night."

"MOM!" I heard the sound of disbelief in his voice as he versed his disapproval. "Don't tell me that you're going to let church and that concert take precedence over being with MaMa Cheree!"

"No, I'm not letting it take precedence. I'm simply getting things in order so that I can go and stay with MaMa Cheree as long as need be after the surgery."

I could sense his unvoiced concern through the silence. No, he couldn't believe that I was letting *anything* keep me from being with my mother right now in this situation. Here was a seventeen-year-old feeling the need to spend precious time with a loved one when his own mother was not even doing the same. How could I explain that for one thing, I was carrying out the role of responsibility that his grandmother had drilled in me, and for another, I was afraid my constant presence might send her a message that I was concerned about the outcome on Monday. My mind told me that this was a conversation for tomorrow afternoon's long ride.

"I understand," Rich finally relinquished. And he did, as much as was possible from an adolescent's standpoint and experience.

Again, I decided the best thing to do was discuss this when we were actually together the next day. Rich was an intelligent young man, and I figured once he had time to sit and think about this for a few minutes, there would be no need for an explanation the next day. Either way, I brought the discussion to a close.

"Okay, here's the deal. We'll leave the church the minute the wedding is over and pick up a burger on the way. How does that sound?"

"Great." The hesitation on his end told me that Rich was already thinking through the logistics. "Mom, I hate for you to have to spend four hours driving when you just came home and you're going to have to go right back on Sunday afternoon."

"I don't mind, Rich. I'm touched that you want to make this effort. It will thrill your MaMa."

"I'm glad. I just couldn't let her go into surgery on Monday and . . . "

"I know, honey. You don't have to say another word."

"Mom, she may never be the MaMa I know again."

Pressured by giant tears, my throat was fighting to keep open. Rich's best friend had a mom with cancer, and he had walked every step of the way with that family. He knew the options and the consequences. I wanted to say that we had nothing to worry about, for I really *wasn't* worried, but I knew that if I opened my mouth, my son might get another message from the tears that were sure to be in my voice.

We hung up, each of us feeling for the other, and both of us praying for the one we loved. I knew that this trip was filling a need for not only Rich, but for my parents as well. And for that reason, it filled a need for me, too. My prayer ended with me thanking God for a son that I did not deserve to go along with a wonderful mother I did not deserve. Some people complained that life was not fair. No, it wasn't always fair, and this was one of those times that I was sure glad it wasn't.

On the way back, Rich and I laughed about all the times we had shared all over the world with his MaMa.

"Mom, how in the world could she walk so fast with such short legs?"

"I don't know, but if there had been a race, she

would have won every time."

Neither of us spoke for a few minutes, each flashing back to our own special memories. I was the one to bring those recollections together.

"What is your first memory of your grandmother?"

"I'm not really sure, Mom." Rich paused briefly, as if trying to pull that particular instance out of a magical hat. A chuckle and a nod of his head told me he had an answer. "The first time I remember traveling with her is the time we went to California to hear Doug sing. While we were in San Diego, she jumped over those posts out on the Boardwalk with us." He paused again, as if drawing in a clearer image. "And we were all doing that Huck Finn hop, kicking our heels up to one side, and then the other. Do you remember?"

"I sure do. It amazed me even then how she put both hands on the posts, and jumped up in the air, straddling the post and running to the next one right behind you and Doug. You couldn't even get up over the top of them, but you sure gave it your all." Now I was the one chuckling and shaking my head. "I can remember thinking back then what a blessing it was for my sons to have Cheree Miller for a grandmother. She was really something special."

There was another pause as we both continued to visualize that bright, sunny summer afternoon down by the Pacific Ocean with surfers and roller bladers all around us.

Rich kept the memories flowing. "That's where we saw the most spectacular sunset we've ever seen. We were sitting in that seafood restaurant that sat out over the ocean eating our salads as the sun started down. It was the first time any of us had been on the West coast and our table was right where we could see out the window. The sun got smaller and smaller until it looked like a layer cake, then a pie, then a pancake, then a pat of butter, and then it was gone."

"Isn't it odd that we've seen so many sunsets together, yet that is the one that sticks out in all our minds?" I questioned, still envisioning that particular scene in my own mind.

"Why is that?" Rich reflected, delving into his own philosophical world more than asking a question.

"Oh, I think it probably had a lot to do with the company, and the fact that it was our very first evening on the Pacific Ocean." I glanced at my son, who was staring out the window at the stars over the mountain, trying to decide whether he was even listening. "Do you know what I remember the best about that trip?"

"No, what?" he asked, still in his own world of memories.

"That trip was the first time MaMa Cheree had ever flown. She always said that the first thing she was going to do when she got me out of college was to fly on an airplane. That wish turned out to be one of those 'round tuits'. When Doug was selected to sing in that national children's choir, I was determined she was going with us. The funny thing is that she did not need any convincing. She didn't even hesitate when I asked her to go." Rich turned his head, tuning into the story and reliving the flight with me. "The flight out there was perfect. There was not a cloud in the sky and no turbulence. We flew over the Grand Canyon and the pilot banked the plane on both sides so that all the passengers could see the beauty below us. It was so clear that I was able to get gorgeous pictures of the canyon from the plane's window. You could even see the white-water ripples in the Colorado River, it was so clear."

"And then there was the flight home," I continued. "You were only five, and you sat in the window seat of the row with me so you could see. MaMa Cheree and Doug sat right in front of us. There were so many tornadoes in the Midwest that the pilot simply could not get over the storm. We had a connecting flight in St. Louis on the way back. Now you have to remember that there was a horrendous crash in Sioux Falls, Iowa, a couple of days after we got to California. In fact, I kept hoping that your grandmother didn't hear about it on the news, but I should have known better than that."

"Was she frightened?"

"No, not a bit. Your Great-Grandma Rose was terrified, and your Great-Uncle Edwin said she'd probably walk home, but it didn't even seem to faze MaMa Cheree. Anyway, as we were landing in St. Louis, I told you and Doug to keep your eyes open so you could see the giant arch. As we were making our descent, a lightning bolt went straight down the side of the plane, right beside you and your brother. I didn't think too much about it, but then as we finally came out of the clouds and the plane was practically on the ground, all we could see was that there was no runway – not even an airport – in sight. The pilot jerked the plane back up just before it touched down, so sharply that it threw everyone straight back in their seats. There was a black lady behind us whose startled voice yelled, 'Oh, dear Jesus.' That seemed the catalyst that got everyone on edge, if the sudden jerk hadn't already. We got back up in the air, came down again, with everyone staring out the windows, hoping and praying for a different vision."

"And?" Rich asked, like a child who knew the ending of the bedtime story, but he just wanted to hear it again.

I gladly obliged him. "And we got a different vision, alright. That time we could see the airport when we came out of the clouds, but no runway. When the pilot pulled us back up a second time, there were some Germans in front of us who joined the black lady's calling on the Lord. The third time we started down, we didn't get quite so close to the ground before the pilot came on and told us that there were bad tailwinds, and that the airport was changing the direction for our landing. Once again we soared up and circled for a few minutes, waiting our turn for clearance. The few minutes turned into half an hour, and the pilot came back on and told us that we were going to have to land in a nearby field. After the crash only a week earlier, the French family behind us joined the cacophony of the Germans and the black lady. White knuckles were visible all the way up the aisles. Everyone was turning around and looking at all the other passengers, wondering about their fates and whether the passengers around them were the last persons they would ever see."

"I glanced up in front of me at MaMa Cheree. I had given her chewing gum to help with her ears on the way down during the first descent, and now she was chewing away, all the color gone from her face. Up until that point, I had been praying, like everyone else on the aircraft, only quieter than our neighbors. After all, I was the seasoned traveler here, and I felt it my duty to keep your grandmother and you guys from being scared. But I must admit that I, too, was more than a little worried about the outcome of our landing. All I could think was that I had brought my mother along for a wonderful trip and flight, and here I was going to kill her. And not only that, but my father's entire family - for here were his only grandchildren and his only child, along with the love of his life. So, changing my silent words at that point, I prayed that if the plane went down, God would just go ahead and take me, for I knew that if I let something happen to his loved ones, your PaPa Mark would kill me when he got his hands on me."

"In the midst of this prayer, your brother turns around and asks in a loud resounding voice, 'Are we going to crash?'"

"I couldn't answer him truthfully because I really had no idea about that myself. But I mustered all the confidence I could and replied with a smile, 'Of course not!' I don't know when I have ever come closer to an Emmy award."

"Then as we began what seemed like a normal descent, except for the fact that the plane was coming down into a field, the plane suddenly took one last pull back up into the air. This time it had been before we got to the ground. The pilot came on and announced, 'Ladies and gentlemen, we have just gotten communication back with the control tower.' All the passengers glared at each other, in total shock that we had been trying to touch down without use of the communication system, or the instrument panel, and that we had truly been at God's mercy in the belly of that big bird – or whale, as you called it later, telling your teacher how we were all like Jonah."

"All of a sudden, even though we had just been told that the emergency was over, every single passenger was praying aloud. Every single passenger, that is, with the exception of your grandmother, your brother, you and me. I'm not too sure that we weren't just afraid to speak, but I was hoping that the three of you were trusting me to keep you safe. I can remember shutting my eyes and praying for Mama and you guys, hoping that Daddy would not be left all alone."

"The plane touched down on the runway and people looked at each other in total amazement and ecstasy. Not until we actually pulled up to the gate did people relax. By that point, they literally had to pry their fingernails out of the arms on the seat."

"When the plane finally came to a complete halt, the entire group of passengers broke into screams, yells and applause. The pilot met each and every passenger on their way out and thanked them for flying with that airline."

"I remember that," Rich nodded. "He pinned the little plastic wings on Doug and me himself. And Doug always laughed and told everybody we had seen the Arch in St. Louis from every angle except upside-down."

"Yes, and that's pretty much the truth!" I concluded the story, remembering the last of the details.

"You know, that flight almost did me in. We were supposed to have ninety minutes to change planes and look around. Instead, by the time the plane landed, we only had eight minutes to catch our next flight. I had sworn during that catastrophe that if I ever got on the ground again, I would never get on another airplane. I was determined to rent a car and drive home, taking no more chances with my mother's life."

"But when we got out of the plane, the rush of the crowd, all individuals trying to make their own connecting flights, pushed us toward our gate. Like sheep following one another, we just kept walking. We had boarded the plane and sat down, neatly arranging all of our carry-ons, which were many back then, before it dawned on me that I had put us right back in harm's way. I guess I was in a state of shock from the near-miss situation."

"No one mentioned what had happened, and your MaMa was still chewing her gum, her skin white as a lamb's wool, making her fit the part of us being herded through the airport. I was afraid she was going to have a stroke, fearing the danger for her was not over yet. Before I had time to think much more about it, the pilot came on and announced that the storm had moved out as quickly as it had moved in and that we had been cleared for take-off."

"The flight attendants had the foresight to serve us immediately. None of us had much to say on that last leg of the flight home. All I can remember is you still playing with your toys, unaware that anything had been in any way out of the ordinary, and the fact that we did not even hit one single bump on the way back to Charlotte. And that I was still praying that God would not let anything happen to my mother."

"I also remember Daddy being there to pick Mama up when we got off the plane. He made small talk about the trip, grabbing both of you guys and hugging you, not aware that there had been any problem whatsoever."

"As we exited the airport, and Mama and Daddy turned toward their car in the parking lot, I pulled her aside and whispered that I hoped she had not gotten scared too badly on the flight from LA. She looked at me with the most nonchalant expression and said, 'Oh, no. I knew the pilot had it all under control. I figured he deals with that kind of stuff every day.'"

"I can remember standing there dumbfounded, watching she and Daddy walk to their car, Mama still chomping on that same piece of gum, and her undaunted faith a glowing part of her. At the time, I don't think I even realized the depth of her statement. It has only been in the years since that I have observed that pure child-like faith in every part of her life."

Rich and I rode in silence for a few miles, both of us trying to grasp the magnitude of that entire trip. From the matchless sunset to the Huck Finn style of kicking our heels up on the Boardwalk. From the streets of Tijuana, Mexico, to the footprints outside Graumann's Chinese Theater. From the rides of Disneyland to the crafts of Knott's Berry Farm. From the baseball game at the Dodgers Stadium to the organ concert in the Crystal Cathedral. From the picture-perfect flight into LAX to the near-miss flight home. The conversation had made us both aware of the most important remembrance from that trip. It had nothing to do with the sights, or the rides, or even the memorable flight.

It was a simple lesson learned from a grandmother. A lesson of love, faith and trust. A lesson that left a grown woman standing dumbfounded amidst the hustling, bustling crowd of an international airport. A lesson that still impacted a daughter and a grandson even twelve years later. A lesson that was still as much a part of my mother today as it was back then.

"Mom, was there ever a time when you saw MaMa Cheree worry?" His voice was soft and full of introspect.

It took little time to think back over the years about that question. "No, I really can't say that I have. I'm sure there had to be times when she wondered about things like everyone else, but I honestly can't say that I have seen her worry. She has always been quiet and kept things to herself, so one never knew what she was thinking. If she was ever worried about her own welfare, it certainly never showed."

"Mom?" The deep thought was still evident in Rich's voice.

"Yes?" I asked, hoping to encourage the impending words.

"I'm so glad you made the effort to take me to see MaMa Cheree. I had to see her . . . to see her one last time . . . you know, in case something went wrong on Monday." There was a pause. I knew better than to break into his thought, letting him piece the words together as they would come. "Even if the surgery went well, I was terrified that I would never see my MaMa again as I know her now, and have known her my entire life. But seeing her bright smile tonight, and that perfect innocence written all over her face, even in the midst of all the tubes going in and out of her body, I realize that she is going to be exactly the same."

My prayer flew up like a missile, asking God not to let my eyes get so blurred from the heavy tears I felt in them that I was unable to see to drive. This child, the same child in whom I had heard such maturity when he called about visiting his grandmother, had just shown me that he was much more of an adult than he was a child. My baby would soon be a man. I braced myself for Rich's next words.

"What makes MaMa MaMa is not her physical appearance. It is her spirit and her will for life. Her joy and her peace. All the wonderful fruits of the Spirit that come from that faith she totes around all the time."

I listened, waiting to see if Rich had any more words of wisdom. He took a deep breath, exhaling as if releasing all the psychological toxins from his body and then concluded, "I just want to know one thing."

"What's that?" I asked, totally unprepared for his next question.

"How is it that someone as tiny as her can cart that much faith around with her all the time?"

I smiled and shook my head, looking over at Rich's face in the darkness. After thanking God for providing me with a way to take care of the tears, I responded. "I guess that's why she's so small. It takes a lot of exercise and energy to carry all of that inside her."

We both laughed, allowing our bodies the release they needed from the trauma that was enveloping us. Rich laid his head back and shut his eyes. I was not sure if he was really tired, or if he simply needed a break from all the memories. Or if he just wanted to relish the ones that were in his mind at the moment.

As he reclined in the passenger seat, I rehashed my own thoughts from that trip. The seafood restaurant in San Diego was now gone. I had tried to find another like it on several recurrent trips since, but to no avail. Although I had sat on the beaches of California on many occasions after that, I never saw the sun go down in the same manner again.

My mind had now wandered into the same deep valley that Rich's had earlier. My thoughts were philosophical and lasting. I contemplated on the fact that one can never truly relive a memory. The memory of an event in your mind is what makes it so special, so extraordinarily awesome. Otherwise, they would be nothing more than the mundane things of everyday life.

I turned to glance at Rich. Even with the maturity he had just displayed, there was a look of total naiveté on his face. Here was a seventeen-year-old that could have spent the evening with his friends or gone on a date with his girlfriend, but he opted to make a long ride just to see his grandmother for a couple of hours. The pride inside was the only thing that kept me from breaking down.

Yes, it was a hardship driving up that mountain, just to drive back down, and then turn around and do it all over again tomorrow. But I had an idea these trips were going to become fairly frequent, and I knew that they were going to remain treasured moments rather than hardships.

One of Rich's remarks from the past shot through

my head. It came on an afternoon when I had planned to take him shopping and we had stopped by MaMa Cheree's to pick up something. He decided that he would rather stay and help his grandmother in her garden than to go shopping with me. It was a regular occurrence for both my sons to want to stay with their grandparents whenever the opportunity arose.

On that particular Saturday, I half jokingly made a comment to the effect that I did not understand why my kids would rather be with their grandparents than their mom.

With no hesitation whatsoever, Rich blurted out, "It's okay, Mom. Your grandchildren will like you best, too!" We had all laughed heartily at his statement. The fact was, that in all the philosophical seriousness a young boy could muster, he had spoken a major truth, even though it had served as a tidbit of humor for the rest of us.

It was odd how I remembered that remark at this particular moment. But looking at Rich's face, a face full of love and devotion to his elders of two generations, I didn't mind that I had come in second-place behind my mom. He was right. I had a suspicion that my grandchildren *would* like me best. And that would be because of all the lessons I had learned from all the generations of grandmothers before me.

It was Mother's Day weekend, and I had just been given the greatest gift of all time. My son, my baby, who would legally become a man in three days on his eighteenth birthday, had reaped his own "fruits of the Spirit." To see that in a child was the greatest gift any mother could receive. I knew I would rest easy that evening, with the knowledge that my son was ready to be a man.

And I looked up at the stars and thanked God for small gardens.

Three

I sat down on one of the concrete benches outside the front entrance of the hospital. Somehow I felt that I wasn't quite ready to make the journey up to Mama's room. The distance was not great, for Pardee was not a large hospital by any means. In fact, Jim and I had made numerous trips in and out and all around it on Friday when we had first come here. But it now seemed that the few steps to the elevator, and then down the second floor hall, were going to be endless.

My mind knew exactly what was going on. It

wasn't the physical aspect of the walk, but solely the mental and emotional strings – tugging, twisting, pulling - getting themselves all tangled around my logical and physical abilities until they were taking over my actions.

Jim looked at me as I sat there, and then glanced to the card in my hand. His eyes told me that he knew what was going on inside of me, and he understood that this was one of those times when I needed a little space. For how long, he didn't know, but he did know that he was going to grant me that time and space, no matter how long it took.

As he kissed me gently on the forehead and walked away, I was given another reminder that we truly had climbed some mountains together and reached some very comfortable plateaus in our marriage. I saw him walk into the front lobby and sit down, picking up a magazine to leaf through as I collected my thoughts and memories. His foresight allowed me to rid myself of all the excess mental and emotional baggage before I went about my mission of being there for my mother.

I knew he could care less about the magazines, like most of the other people who read through them there. In fact, most of the magazines were filled with empty words, but they served a very real purpose. They filled time. They took people's minds off the stress and tension that accompanied the illness of a loved one. They allowed my husband to be just inside the front door where he could keep an eye on me should he decide his presence was needed. They had a very real purpose. *Empty words that speak volumes. What a genius concept.*

My face gave way to a somber smile. *And they gave me a break from the turmoil going on inside my entire body.*

I held up the card, feeling it as if to check its weight, trying to figure out whether it was heavy enough to carry all the love that was attached to the words inside. Although I had spent a good hour choosing that card, it now seemed so insignificant. Every word written on it was true, and meaningful, yet - how could one wrap up a lifetime in that one little envelope?

And for me, it truly *was* a lifetime. For as I sat amidst the flowers of the hospital's garden, the magnitude of this day struck me like bolts of lightning flashing down from the sky, with such a force that they ricocheted off the ground and the trees around me, yet with a softness like the breath of angels sweetly singing in such lush harmonies that it swept away all negativity. I listened as even the birds hushed their singing to hear it, too.

No, I was not crazy. I was not letting my mind run away with itself under the duress of the moment. But I was clearly and visibly in touch with my Maker.

What I was feeling was God's assurance that He *was* right there in the garden with me. And He *was* in that hospital room upstairs on the second floor. And He *was* speaking to my heart through the many voices of nature. And He *was* answering a prayer right before my very eyes and ears. In fact, I realized that all of my senses were tingling with the ambience of the moment. A moment that I knew would pass as quickly as it had come, yet a moment that would carry me for many years, as many years as I was alive.

And I felt an indescribable comfort knowing that what I now felt was the same peaceful presence that Cheree Miller had felt forty-seven years ago today, on the first Mother's Day that she had reason to celebrate the day for herself.

I closed my eyes and envisioned that day – that cold, rainy day that was so out of character for a usually gorgeous warm spring, bursting with sunshine and flowers. But on that particular day, the dampness placed an added chill into the air that was already cold from the elements that had come together to cause the weather to be so unseasonably odd.

My body shuddered as the same chilling dampness ran down my spine and through my bones. It seemed to be heightened by the stark white concrete block walls, and the black-and-white tiles of the floor that I pictured in that hospital.

Suddenly, I felt transported back in time as I saw a doctor, working rapidly and frantically with the aid of several nurses, trying to clear out the passages and the lungs of a newborn infant. The baby was sputtering and coughing, and turning unnatural shades of blue and purple from the congestion caught in its bronchial tubes.

I heard one of the nurses softly whisper to another, "That baby will never make it through the day."

The other nurse pursed her lips and lowered her head, nodding slightly, giving her unspoken agreement to the statement that had just been made.

Machines, all equipment that looked terribly primitive by today's standards, were wheeled into the delivery room while the operators and the doctor took turns giving orders to all the aides around them. As one of the men prepared to take the tiny, frail baby and hook it to the giant, monstrous steel machine, the infant coughed uncontrollably, so hard that it was literally shaking in the hands of the nurse holding it. The blue and purple skin became streaked with splotches of bright yellow, as infection came spewing from the baby's mouth. It sounded as if every thing inside that child was coming out from the force of the coughs that were ejecting continual fluids, while she was swallowing giant gulps of air on the intakes, forcing life back into her lungs.

It appeared that the tiny little baby had taken over control of her own life in the inabilities of all the doctors and nurses surrounding her. The small face, covered in tears from sheer force, and layers of mucous, began to radiate. Nurses quickly wiped the face and body of the small life, wrapping the baby girl in clean, fresh blankets.

The lifeless body from only a few seconds ago had turned into a little ball of life, with giant blue sparkling eyes, still crossed from the light hitting them, but that already spoke of the trauma their short life had experienced. Lungs that had been full only seconds ago had given way to clear cavities now bursting with cries – happy cries declaring, "I am here. I am a gift to human-kind. I have a contribution to make."

I felt a laughter inside my soul as the baby let everyone in the room know that she had earned her laughs and her cries, *and her independence!*, in the few short minutes she had been on the face of the earth.

The entire population of the delivery room broke forth with laughter and cries at the miracle that had just taken place before their eyes. Any of them would have gladly taken credit for what had just happened, but they all knew that none of them could.

It was a power that was not foreign to anyone working in that room. They had seen it on numerous occasions, in various settings, in people of all ages, but it never ceased to bring the same incitement of overwhelming emotions with each experience.

As one of the nurses gently laid the now quiet child in her bed, with all eyes focused on the precious little girl – truly a Mother's Day gift from God – they turned as they heard a panicked gulp behind them. In their awe of the moment, and in watching the blessed event before them, the two orderlies who were moving the mother from the delivery table to a gurney let the wheeled bed slip, and the mother was falling to the floor.

The quick-reflexed doctor pivoted around and caught the mother in mid-air. However, not before he was able to keep his back from breaking under the strain of catching his patient in such an awkward position. While the nurses caught the doctor and braced his fall, the orderlies were able to get the mother, who was just coming out of sedation, laid securely back on the gurney.

Although the celebration was short-lived, not a soul in that room ever forgot the life of the little girl that came into the world that day, nor the events – both good and bad – that surrounded the miraculous occasion.

I felt myself becoming a part of the present again as I slowly opened my eyes and viewed the garden all around me. The vision I had just seen seemed so real, yet here I sat, under the limbs of dogwoods and tulip trees that had given way to the Japanese cherry blossoms all around me. I looked down at my arm. Although the afternoon was glistening with sunlight, my arms were moist from little droplets that felt like fresh morning dew.

My conscious mind knew what had just happened. It was one of those instances that you read about, but you never think much about, in the magazines – the magazines filled with empty words. The ones like Jim was eyeing, unaware of the spiritual gift his wife had just been given. I didn't even bother to look around me to see if others had seen what had gone on around me, for I knew they had not. They had walked on, passing right by me, with no knowledge that anything was out of the ordinary only steps away from them.

I smiled as I looked up at the heavens, then back to the breathtaking array of flowers all around my feet.

Shades of pinks, purples, blues and yellows were touching the day with their vibrant colors, bringing a sense of awe and wonderment to all who witnessed their natural beauty, and an aroma of peaceful joy that lingered loftily in the air.

My attention turned back to the card in my hand. I wondered if my mother even had an idea of all that had happened on the day I was born. She knew that the doctor had been hospitalized for six weeks after my birth, for she and Grandma Rose went back to visit him and thank him for the infant he had brought into the world. But as far as all the other events, I had my doubts. She knew that I was full of congestion, and I had heard the stories passed on to her from the nurses. But I seriously doubted she had been given all the ensuing details.

Regardless, I knew that God had seen fit to work a miracle on that Mother's Day forty-seven years ago, that He had allowed a mother to hold onto her blessed child. Now I was praying that God would once again use this setting to work another Mother's Day miracle. Only this time, I was hoping that He would allow the child to hold onto her blessed mother.

As I finished my prayer, a vision came to me of another prayer once spoken in a garden – a vision of a lone, solitary man, kneeling beneath the olive trees, also not wanting to drink from the cup. *God, grant me the serenity to accept the things I cannot change*, I whispered as I stood to take the card to my mother.

Four

$\mathcal{A}$quick glance at my watch told me that we had been sitting in the waiting room for just over the ninety minutes that Dr. Stallings had projected for the surgery. Daddy and Jim had been involved in avid conversation earlier, but both had retreated to the daily newspaper. I would have taken bets that Daddy did not remember one word that he had read.

Like anyone else that had ever sat in a waiting room, every minute past the prescribed time seemed to take longer and longer. I wondered how long it would be before Daddy looked up at the wall clock and said something about the time. Not an athletic fan, I had no idea what was in the sports section of the paper, but I hoped it was enough to hold his attention for a while longer. The comics and obituaries had already exhausted their capacity.

I continued to try to make words on my computer, but now with little avail, for diverting my attention to the patient in front of me instead of the one back in surgery. My eyes danced over to Jim to see if he had also noticed the time. As I figured, he had, and was returning my glances, alerting me to the fact that he was also focused on my father's well-being for the moment.

As badly as I wanted something to drink, I was not about to move, afraid that my action might stir Daddy's attention. I appreciated the fact that it was also way past time for Jim's coffee cup to be refilled. Both of us went back to trying to stay busy, him reading empty words, me typing empty words.

My mind replayed the morning's scene with Dr. Stallings as he came and spoke to Mama in her room, and then to us in the waiting area before the surgery. He and Dr. Atkins had carefully studied the test results from Friday's colonoscopy, and had a well-planned strategy against the enemy. They had called in three reinforcements, one being from their own practice, one an urologist. and another specialist in reconstructive surgery. I didn't know whether to be calmed by the fact that the three long-time partners were joining forces in my mother's battle, or frightened by the fact that her condition required that much brain, skill, and manpower.

I could see him in his street clothes, smiling with the energy and excitement of a five-year-old boy, with eyes that danced and sang of his love for his patients, but that also spoke of a deep desire to help mankind. He took my mother's hand, leaned over her, and said, "Bless your sweet little heart."

Bless your sweet little heart. Right off the bat, I felt the barricade of anxiety have a huge section blown out of it. For here was a doctor who knew blessings. Here was a doctor who knew the source of blessings. Here was a doctor who recognized the fact that he was working on a woman dear to her family and loved ones. Here was a doctor who possessed a bedside manner that spoke of care and concern. Here was a doctor who knew his stuff, both for the patient in the bed, and the patients standing beside the bed.

He had disappeared just before the nurses came to take my mother to the surgical suite and direct us to the waiting room. Then, shortly after Daddy, Jim and I got settled in the waiting area, the volunteer receptionist came and said that Dr. Stallings and Dr. Atkins would like to see us in one of the family rooms. She led us a few short steps to a side room and had us sit. The two doctors came in, fully robed in their green attire, missing only their gloves and masks.

Dr. Atkins shook hands with us, seeming like an old friend just since Friday. "We've gone over the test results several times, and as I told you on Friday, this malignancy is quite extensive. We are hoping that it is contained in the rectum, but we certainly have no guarantees. What really scares us is how close it is to the bone, and whether it is actually attached, as it appears to be from the pictures."

I stared at Daddy. He was listening intently, his expression never changing, determined not to miss as much as a syllable by his failing sense of hearing. I could catch Jim's stare on me out of the corner of my eye. We each had a personal care partner, and yet, a team.

Dr. Stallings took his turn. "While we have her open, we are going to take lymph nodes from several other areas to check for other dangers. We have three other doctors helping us, all very reputable surgeons, all familiar with her test results, who will be assisting in the surgery. Please know that we are going to do everything possible to get it all."

His words of encouragement were appreciated, but I remembered all too well the statement from Dr. Atkins on Friday. *There's just no easy way to put this.*

My mother had been overtaken by an alien, a terrorist, a murderer. It had encamped inside her body. I knew what was at risk, and so did these doctors. Daddy, Mama and I had not had this conversation, but it was one of those things that needed no words.

Dr. Atkins assured us that either he or Dr. Stallings would be out as soon as the surgery was over to talk with us, probably in this same room. Then Dr.

Stallings said something I will never forget. "Why don't we have a prayer together?"

We all followed his lead and bowed our heads. Although it had only been two hours since that happening, I could not recall the exact words of the prayer. For it was not the surgeon's words that were important. It was the words of the Great Physician speaking through him that I heard. For what I heard was, *Here is a doctor that knows the Greatest Physician – he knows the Greatest Physician by name. Here is a doctor that knows his human limitations – he knows where those limitations stop and the Great Physician takes over. Here is a doctor who never goes into surgery alone – he always has an extra pair of Eyes, of Hands. Here is a doctor who has heard the prayers of this family – he has heard them many times before. Here is a doctor who will give his all to save a life – he will give his all to the One who saved his life.*

The barricade inside my consciousness, which had only been damaged earlier, was now completely destroyed. And here I sat, a part of me screaming to be antsy, to be on the edge of my seat, and another part feeling absolutely no anxiousness at all, having that prayer – those words I could not even remember – to keep me filled with a peace that surpassed all understanding.

Daddy looked up from his paper and glanced in my direction. I quickly opened the conversation, not wanting him to get a chance to worry. "Can I get you some more coffee, Daddy? Or how about some cookies?

They just put a whole basket of Lorna Doones on the counter beside the coffee pot."

My love for cookies came from my father, so I knew that was a safe bet for a needed distraction.

"Sure, I'll have some cookies and some more coffee."

I caught the look of satisfaction on Jim's face, relieving withdrawal signs from his own lack of morning caffeine. I also caught the glance of Daddy's eyes toward his watch. He didn't make a sound, and I sighed silently inside.

Daddy was opening his mouth to make some sort of comment as I caught a glimpse of Doug's car out the front window. We all headed toward the window to watch for him to come into the hospital. All talk turned to my son's good nature, his grades, and how proud we were of his latest accomplishment, being named president of the Student Government. I had been glad that he had summer school earlier this morning so that he hadn't had to sit in the waiting room, but at the moment, I was thankful that he didn't have afternoon classes. His appearance immediately brightened Daddy's spirit as they immediately went into a discussion of the previous night's baseball game.

Thank God somebody in the family shares Daddy's interest in sports!

I knew we were good for another hour, not expecting to need it. But as the second hand of the clock approached 11:30, four hours from the start of the surgery, my own clock started ticking, fearing that my mother's surgery had been much more complicated that what even the surgeons had suspected. My panic button had not gone off, for the calm that I had reached both by my two-hour walk with my Father on Friday night, combined with Dr. Stallings' earlier prayer, had me in a worry-free zone. But there was still some major concern for my father, and I would have liked to have some information as to what was taking so much longer than expected.

Daddy's internal alarm must have also gone off, for at that exact moment, he looked down at his watch and looked around at us with a questioning gaze. "What do you think is taking so long?" He looked back at the hands on his timepiece, and you could watch his mind calculating the length of time it had been since the surgery began. His eyes again searched our faces for answers we could not give. "I hope nothing's wrong." I could detect the already present worry creeping into his voice, more audibly with each word.

"I'm sure everything's fine, Daddy. They are probably just taking their time and being extremely thorough. Besides, you know the saying, 'No news is good news.' I'm sure that if there were any need to worry, one of the doctors would have been out here to see us earlier. Mama is in good hands."

He nodded, looking at Jim and Doug for assurance, which he got.

I put my hand on top of his, and looked straight

into his eyes. "And you know that she really *is* in the *best* of Hands."

"Yes, I do know that. What about Dr. Stallings praying with us? That was awfully nice of him. Have you ever known a doctor to do that before?"

"I have seen one, and heard of only a handful that have done that. I must admit that it made me feel a whole lot better, too."

Daddy busied himself telling Doug all about the doctor's words, while I looked at Jim with a wonderment of my own.

A familiar voice turned our attention as it called out to my father. "Hello, Mark. I wondered if you would still be down here." The man addressing Daddy turned and spoke to Doug and me, also extending his hand to Jim, introducing himself.

I had met this man briefly on one other occasion, so at least I had recognized him. But now as I watched him sit down beside my father and engage himself in a conversation that went through stages - from my mother's condition, to other members of their class, to concerns of the church, to areas of common interest – I knew why he was so popular among his peers.

This man, Earl Gates, who happened to be my parent's Sunday School teacher, possessed a hospital visitation demeanor that was void of most learned ministers I knew. In the short span of time he had been here, he had shown concern to my mother and her entire family, he had given my father an opportunity to care about others, and he had dovetailed his past with my father's past, giving them a mutual connection.

Watching him with Daddy, I saw something else, another blessing that had been in the making all around me during that morning. My parents had spent their entire lives in church, yet there was no minister with them during this ordeal. The senior pastor was in the midst of moving and was away, and the associates were all involved in something that had called them away – an odd occurrence for such a large downtown congregation. So, it had fallen the duty of this man to come and sit with my father – a job that he would have done anyway. The doctor had come in to pray with my mother, then my family – a simple act, which eluded to the fact that my mother's future lay in a man of faith, a most rewarding thought.

What was so amazing here is that you expect a minister to come and pray with you, for you know that person is of God. But when a doctor, the one who is truly *the* instrument in such a time, prays for and with the family, there *is* a gift, there *is* an unexpected odd in the patient's favor. And as I watched Earl speaking with my father, his every move focused on Daddy's words and mannerisms, I realized that this was the man for the job.

No wonder his reputation preceded him. I had no doubts that Earl was every bit the teacher that my parents had raved about. But more amazing, he was the minister, the unannounced minister, that truly *did* possess the gift of healing for his flock. How blessed were the people who were fortunate to know the talent of this man. And how blessed were we that this man, and Dr. Stallings, were the ministers that God had sent to Cheree and Mark Miller. *And me.*

The phone rang, and our whole party jumped. I knew it was the call we had been waiting for. Obviously, from the look on their faces, so did everyone else.

"Yes, they're right here." The receptionist was looking in our direction, verifying our suspicions. She moved over to get us, but we had all already started collecting our things, and were out of our seats by the time she got to where we were seated. "Dr. Stallings will be right out to speak with you," she stated, directing us to the same room where the surgeon had prayed.

The doctor came in right behind us, still clothed in green scrubs, this time without the long-sleeved coat. *Mama must have given them quite a work-out*, I mused, noticing the change in his dress. I knew she had won this battle from the lack of distress in Dr. Stallings' face.

"She did great, just great." The sighs of relief filled the small room, as Daddy lost countless pounds off his shoulders. "We were able to get every bit of the malignancy, and even though it was right up against the bone, we were able to get it." This time there was no hidden, 'but.' Only a continual outpouring of all the results and the expected foresightable future, both short-term and long-term. He went on to describe exactly how extensive the damage to the other areas of her abdomen was, but assured us that the infantry of five doctors had been able to effectively battle every one of them. They had restructured much of her lower abdomen, and taken twenty-samples from lymph nodes, making sure they had successfully wiped out the enemy.

"This was truly nothing less than a miracle – one of the greatest we have ever seen. Let's all join in a prayer of thanks."

Again, we lowered our heads with this man, who gave honor and praise to the Hands who had truly performed the surgery. I listened intently, but as before, I heard only the voice of the Great Physician. *Here is a minister, a healer, a messenger, an instrument, my child, your brother. You are blessed, my child.*

Dr. Stallings spoke to us individually, shaking hands with each one, then giving the invitation to call if there were any questions or problems, letting us know that he, or one of his colleagues, would be by twice a day to check on my mother's condition. The surgeon left us alone to laugh, cry, shout, talk, pray – whatever we wished – for a few minutes before we needed to leave the room. He had indicated that it would be at least another hour-and-a-half before my mother came out of recovery. The extensive surgery had taken much anesthesia, so they were not planning to let her go too soon.

Earl prayed once more with all of us before leaving three generations of love to sort through the reality of all that had happened in less than a week's span. He, as well as knowing what to say, knew when to leave. *God's messengers have perfect timing.*

Daddy took out a handkerchief, wiped the tears of joy and blew his nose. Doug hugged Jim and me before grabbing his PaPa. Jim put his arm around me and gave me the most understanding smile I had ever seen. And I thought of the doctor's words.

This was truly nothing less than a miracle – one of the greatest we have ever seen.

A miracle. One of the greatest we have ever seen. One.

I knew this was one of two miracles. For this miracle had a twin, forty-seven years earlier. It, too, had been delivered by a doctor in a hospital. It, too, had been one of the greatest ever seen. It, too, had shaped the lives of two women – separately . . . and together.

A miracle – a baby. A miracle – a mother. Thanks be to God.

The men were jabbering non-stop, all basking in the glory of their miracle. None of them were aware of the double miracle. Daddy had been in the Navy, so he had missed all of the excitement with the first miracle. I held a blessing in my heart, in my soul, that could never be fully described. These three men had heard the good news from the physician. But I had heard the Good News from the Physician.

I looked at them, knowing they were as much in a state of shock as I was, although from different sources. "Those egg salad sandwiches in the gift shop sure sound good," I said, ready to head them away from the waiting area.

"I guess I am ready to eat something. What time

is it?" Daddy looked at his watch. Blessed was this child, too, that he had not even the foggiest notion of how long the surgery had actually lasted until this moment.

We sat down to a wonderful meal, wonderful fellowship, and wonderful communion, enjoying all that the gift shop in a small town hospital could offer – which in the town of Hendersonville, North Carolina, happened to be a lot.

After we filled ourselves with a plentiful dose of nourishment to get us through the long afternoon and evening ahead, I excused myself to replenish my spiritual nourishment – in the garden.

Today's call to Aunt Louise was much different from the one on Friday. I was anxious to make this one, knowing she was probably sitting by the phone, awaiting any news at all. I prayed that her years of experience as a hospital nurse would keep her from worrying needlessly, but I had the foresight to know how people in the medical field were when it came to their own family members. As a rule, they were not able to deal well with that situation. My aunt was no different. It was difficult for her years of professional experience to take over her natural-born older-sibling role.

I went through every detail of the morning, then the doctor's report, word for word. She questioned me several times, not wanting to miss any part. I was sure that she was putting the pieces together in her mind, making it as real to her imagery as possible in her need to feel her nearness to Mama's presence.

The conversation ended with her in a flood of tears, wishing she could physically be there, glad for the outcome, fearful of the future, anxious for May 26th to arrive, her mind racing through all sorts of variables, trying to make something sensible come out of all of them.

I assured her that everyone was fine, and that God had truly worked a miracle – even in the words of the surgeons – and that Mama had many wonderful providers of first-rate attention, as did Daddy and the rest of us. The shakiness in her voice was settling.

"Can you order some flowers for her from me? I'll put the money in the mail today."

"Sure. I'll be glad to."

"Is there a really good florist? I want something real pretty, with lots of bright colors. Maybe with some tulips and daffodils. Something she can keep for all the time after she goes home. Something to help remember me, and to know I'm thinking about her."

"There's a florist whose work I admired earlier today. I'll call them and see if they can do something artificial for you."

"That's great. And don't worry about how much

it costs. I want it to be nice."

"I'll be glad to take care of it, Aunt Louise."

"Thanks. Call and let me know how much it is, and if they can get it today or tomorrow." I could hear the pain in her voice, and it hurt me to know how badly she wanted to be with her sister right then. But I knew that she would be needed more later, and I really didn't want her to see Mama this way. I wasn't sure she could handle getting off the airplane and seeing her baby sister, her Cheer, this way. "And, Rosemary, there's one more thing."

"Yes, Aunt Louise?"

"Could you see if maybe they have a pod of red pepper to put in the flowers somewhere?"

I laughed. What a great sense of humor my family was blessed with. I knew that little extra would be a dead giveaway when Mama saw the flowers.

"I'll tell you what. I'll ask the florist, but if she doesn't have anything, I'll go by the grocery store and pick up a couple of pods and get the florist to wire them into the arrangement. How's that?"

"That'll be just fine."

As I hung up the phone, I gave a huge sigh. I wasn't sure whether the pod of red pepper was more for Mama or Aunt Louise. But it didn't matter, for the thought of it had gladdened my aunt's heart. I had heard her laugh as we exchanged our good-byes, so there was healing from it five-hundred miles away.

I shook my head, awed by the fact that so much

healing could come from such a tiny object that was
found (but where else) in the garden.

Five

$\mathcal{D}$addy's call was completely unannounced, but came right on cue as if it had been perfectly scheduled.

"The cancer doctor is coming in this afternoon to talk to us."

"Did he give you a time?" I asked, stopping in my tracks, lest I miss a single detail.

"All he said was sometime between two and four."

"Jim gets off at two and we'll come straight there."

"You don't have to go to that trouble."

Daddy's words said one thing, but his voice gave a completely different message. I had promised him that I would come back when the oncologist came to talk to Mama and him, and I had no intention of breaking that promise. Even though he was feeling very confident with the doctor's reports thus far, I knew that he was still a little gun shy after that first surgery.

"Let's just hope he gets caught up with another patient and is typically late, and we'll get there as fast as we can," I responded, having calculated the two-hour drive in my head.

Since I expected to hear Daddy once again tell me that I didn't need to be there, I was shocked to hear a barely audible, "Please hurry," on the other end of the line. Never in all my years had I heard my father need me. And even if he had, he would have never asked for my help. But to hear him request my presence, in a voice with a slight quiver to it, made my mind up before I hung up the phone.

"Jim Ellis, please."

"Just a minute, Mrs. Ellis. How is your mother doing today?"

I was gratified that Jim had taken the time to include my mother in his conversations at work. For whatever reason, it showed that we were important to him, and in his thoughts when he was away from home. There was a comfort in knowing that he didn't think of us only when it was a necessity. "She's doing very well. Right now, it's my dad I'm more concerned about."

"Is he sick, too?"

"Oh, no. He's having to tread through a lot of foreign territory right now, and I just worry about him."

"I understand. Let me get Mr. Ellis for you."

The short conversation with the receptionist served a valuable purpose for me. It alleviated the fear that Jim was going through the motions of fulfilling the obligation I had requested at the time of his proposal. The fact that he had shown concern at work showed me that there was more here than an old promise.

"Hello."

"Hi, honey."

"What's wrong?"

Was my voice as readable as my father's? "Nothing's wrong. It's just that . . ."

He cut me off before I could finish. "Rosemary, I can hear an apprehension in your voice. Is your mother okay?"

"I think she's fine. Daddy just called to tell me that the cancer doctor is coming in this afternoon, and well . . . " I found myself fighting tears suddenly.

"Come and get me."

"I can do this by myself. It's just that . . ." Again I struggled, but forced myself to go on. "Daddy ended the call with 'please hurry.'"

"Weren't you always taught to mind your parents?"

I could already feel the tension in my body easing.

"Now get out of there, come by and pick me up and let's get to your mother's room before the doctor does."

Jim's words told me that there was no room for argument, and that just as I had felt the urge to be there for my father, so he felt the urge to be there for me.

"I love you," I ended, hearing the same words come through the phone before he clicked down the receiver.

I closed my eyes for an instant, catching my composure and thanking God for such an awesome blessing, all at the same time. It had been one thing to have parents that were always there for me, but to now have a companion, not only there for me, but to be by my side so that I could return the favor of being there for my parents. Words eluded me as I accepted that God was hearing the beatings of my heart, and that He knew that language.

We raced through the hospital as if there were a dire emergency, but in my mind, after the last words from my father's mouth, there was. Jim kept by my side as I briskly made my way through the halls towards Mama's room.

I pushed the door open, knocking as I went, only to find the doctor seated by the bed.

He rose, extending his hand. "Hi. I'm Dr. Fisher. I just finished introducing myself to your parents."

"Dr. Fisher, this is our daughter, Rosemary, and our son-in-law, Jim."

My father was being that Southern gentleman again, but what really touched me was his choice of words in introducing my husband. 'Son-in-law' seemed so much more personal, and had an ownership to my parents as well as me. I wondered if Jim picked up on that, too, or if it was simply a female thing. Either way, I intended to express my sentiments about that to him as soon as we got out of the room.

The doctor shook both our hands, then sat back in the chair. I positioned myself beside Daddy, who was on the opposite side of Mama from the doctor, as Jim took his place beside me.

"I'm glad you will hear this with your parents. The more ears in an instance like this, the better. It some-times seems like a lot to digest at one time. If any of you have a question along the way, stop me and ask."

It struck me that Dr. Fisher spoke to all of us, and not just Mama. He genuinely displayed his appreciation of family and their support.

"The surgeons feel they have gotten all of Mrs. Miller's cancer. From what I understand, this was a complicated surgery, and you are a most fortunate woman." At this point, his eyes were glued on my mother as he leaned over and took her hand. "You look well, and the surgeons tell me that you were an ideal patient."

Pride was bursting inside me. *That attitude thing really works*, I beamed, already sure of that fact from my own experience.

"I've looked over all your charts and all the results, and I feel good that they did, in fact, get the cancer. However, one can never be really sure."

All of a sudden, the security inside me began to slowly melt. I could sense what was coming, and I knew that Cheree's reaction was going to be the same as mine. The unspoken "but" was impending in the doctor's next sentence, and the words that followed it were sure to include radiation and chemotherapy.

I knew my mother well enough to know that the rest of this conversation was probably going to be a waste of time. Somehow, I could not see her going through that ordeal. She had made up her mind long ago that if she was ever diagnosed with cancer, they would not put a knife to her.

But as I stood there, looking at her and at the doctor, I realized that Mama had already gone under the knife. She had been given her options less than a week ago, and she had made her own decision. I decided to quit trying to guess the consequences, and instead, to take in all the facts the doctor could throw at us.

"After examining your records and looking at your past and your excellent health other than this problem, the chances of this never happening again are sixty percent."

I felt a silent sigh from the cheering squad and three anvils go sailing across the room.

"However . . ."

There was that word again. The one word that sent the anvils hurling back at us like boomerangs.

". . . sometimes there are a few cells that are still floating around, and we want to make sure that if there are any, they do not spread to any other areas. The surgeons took samples from twenty-two lymph nodes and other areas of your body and they all look clean. But again . . ."

There was the "but" I had been waiting for.

". . . one can never be too sure. My recommendations are . . ."

I collected my mental pen and paper and began taking notes.

". . . two months of chemotherapy once a week for eight weeks, then six weeks of radiation, taken daily, five days a week." Then looking at us as if to reassure any fears, "Or as Mrs. Miller can stand it," his eyes returning to Mama, "to be finished off by two more months of chemo, again taken once a week."

I glanced down at my mother, trying to read an answer from her, but her expression gave no indication of one. She looked her usual pleasant self, only a little more intent as she was giving the doctor her full attention. But I knew my mother well enough to know that she was wondering what was going through all of our heads. And I also knew her well enough to know that she was going to make up her own mind about this decision. Or at least I hoped that was the case.

No one said anything as Dr. Fisher looked around the room at us, surveying our expressions – not to see if our faces offered an opinion, but to see if we had understood his statements thus far. Satisfied that we were all on the same page, he instructed my mother to have one of us call his office and make an appointment for one week later.

"That should give you time to talk and mull over things."

I got the feeling that what Dr. Fisher considered mulling over things was not exactly what Mama considered mulling over things.

My brain had been taking in every word that the doctor spoke, intent on not missing anything at all, but my eyes had been listening in another way. They searched Dr. Fisher's face, his mannerisms and his expressions, watching for any signal that he was not who I wanted to be making these decisions for my mother.

What I discovered were lightly-colored steel blue eyes that could have been rather hard and harsh - downright cold in their stare. But rather than that, they spoke tenderly of real concern for fellowman, and God's gentle hand of healing. This man had seen God's mercy.

I had heard of some patients asking doctors about their belief in a greater power, but that was unnecessary in this case. Besides the emotion radiating from his eyes, Dr. Fisher's face showed a confidence and a wisdom that was not customary on the face of many doctors.

To make sure we were perfectly comfortable with the recommendations he had made, Dr. Fisher finally concluded, "Are there any questions?" He slowly looked around at each one of us, not rushing us in the least. Then he glued his eyes on my mother. "Good. Then I'll look forward to seeing you, Mrs. Miller, next week." He paused, moving on to the next segment of the report. "Let me explain the various types of treatment."

The doctor explained every single detail about the particular type of chemo he recommended for my mom, alleviating the many fears that it was anything like she had watched people suffer through in the past decades. He described the entire process of what would happen when she entered his office, the symptoms she might experience, and the pitfalls along the way.

I was pleased that he could give the information straight, yet smile the whole time he was talking to Mama. It was obvious that he had presented all of this information on countless occasions before, yet not one time did he recite it to us as if he were simply giving this speech by rote. Dr. Fisher spoke in such a peaceful, tranquil voice that I had no fears of what he was prescribing for her follow-up care.

He had presented the facts so clearly that there was hardly any way that his patients could be left with questions, or fear of the unexpected. While he did not mince words, the calmness of his voice, combined with his amiable bedside manner, proved to dissipate the qualms of the unknown. His words were directed to Mama, yet he glanced at us with each important bit of information so that we all felt a part of the discussion. It was clear that he truly *did* want there to be a well-educated support group for his patient.

As I listened to him give his concluding recommendations, it struck me most odd that this man, much like a commander-in-chief who had come in to plan the attack on an invading terrorist, gave one the feel of a parent who was preparing a child for their first injection, cuddling the child lovingly in his arms and speaking in soothing tones that told the little tyke that everything was going to be alright.

The softness in his eyes turned to a gentle brightness as he gathered Mama's records, stood and once again offered his hand to each of us. We all watched him walk out the door, none of us about to be the first to speak.

When the quiet began to turn to discomfort, Daddy decided to plunge ahead. "Well, he certainly did seem to have it all together, didn't he?"

I felt it my duty to answer so as not to disrupt

Mama's thoughts. "Yes. I'm sure glad we got here when we did."

"Me, too. Cheree was hoping you would be here in time to hear what he had to say."

That fact made me even more grateful we had left immediately after the phone call. But I wasn't as sure that my mother cared about my physical presence as much as she did not want to have to repeat the ordeal herself. I suspected the latter was the case, but it did not matter. I was there. Jim was there. And Mark had an added strength through our presence.

Mama spoke in her normal quiet, yet nonchalant voice. "Show Rosemary and Jim the book about Dr. Fisher," she directed to Daddy. Then turning to us, "He taught classes on oncology at Yale University before coming here to practice."

As I thumbed through the directory of physicians, also noting the surgeons and specialists who had worked on Mama only two days before, I found myself suddenly overjoyed that my parents had retired to the 'number one' retirement community in the country. Their small town had an abundance of reputable doctors, all from the finest schools with all kinds of degrees. But more than that, I had been impressed by the bedside manner of each of the doctors with whom we had come in contact during the past week.

I laid the book down beside the other directory in the room – the directory of the Great Physician.

Six

$\mathcal{M}$ama was thrilled to be home and back in her own space. Her attitude of a gracious care receiver was still difficult for me to appreciate, for she had always been the caregiver. I found it strange that she had accepted this role so easily, having always been so self-reliant. Yet, with the same radiant smile that she did everything else, it was apparent that she was not giving in to the battle that had brought itself upon her unannounced, but rather, was taking a furlough to regroup and come back even stronger than before.

She had never been one to lounge around the house. Therefore, I knew she did not have a wardrobe of gowns and housecoats. And her usually small feet were so swollen that we could barely get socks on them, much less shoes. Here sat my mother in her chair, a distant sight from the appearance of a tiny Geisha doll that she usually seemed.

I looked at her, not with pity in my eyes, but pride in the fact that she still carried the grace of a kindly, graceful Southern woman. In my eyes, she was the most beautiful female creature I had ever seen. She was even more beautiful than at my wedding when she wore the long, powder blue dress, whose shimmering fabric had matched the glow of her eyes in such a way that, combined with the size 2 of her dress, she truly did look like a porcelain Geisha doll.

There was only one thing for me to do. The minute I got her comfortable in her chair, and wrapped in her favorite warm afghan, I excused myself and went to the nearest mall. No discount garbs for my 'queen mother.'

I laughed as I thought of the "Queen for a Day" show that we had watched each afternoon while I was growing up. Little had I realized until this very moment that my own mother, the simple, yet brilliant woman, who had given up a wonderful executive career with a national firm to stay home and raise me, was *truly* a queen. She had been a queen, not for a day, but for everyday of my life.

Even in those years of having to discipline me, it was with pure wisdom and true understanding. No, she was not the iron-clad ruler, but instead, one that looked down from her throne to her subjects with sincere love and care, wishing a good life for all of them – which, in my case, happened to be only one.

I thought about my cousins who used to spend weeks with me during the summer. They, too, were graced by the same keen knowledge of life that I received. Mama had never shown prejudice toward me in arguments, or given in to my wishes over theirs. The sense of a slight "it's not fair" syndrome that I used to feel during their visits now became an awareness of deep gratitude and respect. For I saw how this woman, whose weight only hit three digits when she was soaking wet, was wholly a Christ-like woman. She had ruled her home as Christ had ruled his kingdom. I smiled. *And yes, for those times that I misbehaved like the moneychangers at the temple, she pulled out the green belt!*

The first item of agenda when I returned would be to read the passages from Proverbs that so aptly fit my mother. She had been honored, long before her time, to have joined the countless throng of women who had also followed that guide for womanhood and motherhood that had been outlined so many centuries ago.

But for now, the only thing on my agenda was to find a department store that carried two beautiful gowns and robes and a pair of Velcro slippers befitting of my mother's queenly state.

Once Mama was settled in her own bed for the first night since her surgery, my aching body surrendered to its yearning to make me aware of my physical needs, namely sleep. Even the walk downstairs to the guest room seemed like miles as my tired, limp legs felt the weight of the burden that was piercing me from the inside.

Not sure if I would have to get up during the evening with Mama, I opted to lay down in my comfortable clothes, ready to be upstairs at a moment's notice should I need to play nurse.

The firm mattress from my great-grandmother's rope bed screamed a welcome that was felt throughout my body. As my eyes adjusted to the darkness, the moon shining in between the shades lighted the room enough that the pieces of furniture took the shape of silhouettes against the wall. Even with my eyes closed, I could sense the presence of family pieces from as many as five generations surrounding me, as if each piece of furniture took on a personality all its own.

With my body begging to disregard the familiar feelings and just go to sleep, my brain began to interact with the signals that were now bouncing off the walls, making me aware that I was not alone in this battle against my mother's enemy. Not one to get caught up in the taboo of séances and such, I did not quite understand the feeling of spirits in the room around me. But the faith engrained within me from many generations had given way to the belief that there literally were angels out in the everyday world. So, it did not seem odd to me at all that I felt warmly surrounded by the spirits of Mama's family that had passed on to the afterlife.

My brain won this bout as I stepped into my slippers and made my way over to an antique bookcase lining one of the walls. I recognized it as being the one that had sat in my father's office for several years before his retirement.

Lifting the glass door of the bottom shelf, I turned on the reading lamp with my other hand. The titles of the books were all familiar, some dating back to the Zane Grey westerns of my paternal grandfather's, some the textbooks from my college days, and others as recent as the childhood storybooks of my own children. It struck me that the account I was living was worth more than any that were contained in the books I was admiring, for just looking at the spines in the bookcase told a story of my heritage and of these spirits that I felt were in the room with me.

Curious as to the rest of the contents of the bookcase, I proceeded to lift the door of the spacious top shelf. Its contents were even more reminiscent of my own life as I saw my first-grade reader and my preschool storybooks, some with covers missing from years of daily use. I pulled out one of the earlier storybooks to view my childhood attempts at art, where brightly colored pages gave testimony to a vivid imagination that had taken flight nearly half a century before, when I had drawn pictures in the inside covers and pages. A smile broke across my face as I saw the orange outline of a simply-drawn dog. I turned the page to reveal a brown house with two parents and a child standing in front of it, a bright yellow ball for the sun with short thin lines pointing out from it, green trees, and pink, purple, yellow and blue flowers along the front of the house.

Has every boy or girl ever born drawn this same picture at some point in his or her childhood?

I thought about the spirits in the room with me and wondered how many of them, as children, had envisioned the same image of their household, only with differently shaped houses, and farm animals, and whatever else was common from their lifestyles and time periods.

My mind went back to my drawings as I fondly remembered the little red-leather rocking chair, with the floral tapestry print embossed in the fabric, in which I had sat as a child. It was there that I listened to Mama read to me, and pretended I was reading myself, all the while coloring the pictures. I could still see the old cheap cardboard cigar box that housed my crayons, and the big pasteboard tissue box from the grocery store that sat in the closet and housed the cigar box and all my other toys.

What a simple life!

I chuckled lightly and shook my head at the realization of how beautiful that simple life truly had been.
My parents had never succumbed to the temptations of
the material world during all their years together. And
now it struck me as how ironic it was that here in the
beautiful autumn of their lives, they owned a beautiful
home in the retirement Mecca of the country - a small
town where there was claimed to be more millionaires
per capita than in any other city in the United States.

Yes, simple life truly does reap great rewards. I smiled,
proud of the accomplishments of my parents from their
unassuming lives, as I replaced the storybook and continued to check out the contents in the rest of the bookcase.

Every book that had meaning in my life was
neatly arranged on that shelf, commemorating the life
and times of Rosemary Miller Ellis. Being the organized
retired librarian that Mama was, I was almost surprised
that she had not labeled the shelf as such.

My eyes wandered from spine to spine, searching for more sparks of interest from my past, until they
stopped at two books side by side - the Bible story book
that I had gotten on my fifth birthday, and a picture scrapbook from my growing-up years. Not sure which one to
pull out first, I grabbed both of them and sat down in
the rocking chair beside the reading lamp.

I held the books for a minute, anxious to see their
familiar contents after so many years, but taking in slow

breaths as if conditioning myself for an endurance race. The pages of the two books in my lap were sure to occupy me for a long while, for they held eighteen years of my own past, not to mention the generations before me.

My eyes closed, not from lack of sleep, but trying to help me concentrate and focus on the many memories, and to hold in every one of them. Still feeling the presence of the spirits of my ancestors, I took in one last long deep breath. My own spell was broken as I heard the springs in the bed from the floor above me creak. Unsure as to whether Mama needed to get up, I rushed up the stairs to her room to see her propping herself up on the side of the bed.

"I'm okay," I heard from her faint voice.

"Glad to hear it, but I'm going to help you anyway. This bed is a lot farther from the floor than the one at the hospital, and there are no rails to help balance and support you."

"I can make it. You really don't need..."

"Now, Mama. Would you let me get out of bed by myself if I had just come home from such extensive surgery?"

I saw a smile in the dim glow from the nightlight that told me her answer. My mother had been with me after several surgeries, so she did not offer to make another comment.

She held onto my arm as we made our way to the bathroom. Her reluctance gave way to the understanding that I was simply giving back a small part of all she had given to me all these many years.

"I didn't want to wake you."

"Oh, you didn't," I assured her, then wishing I had not tried to comfort her in that manner, for I knew she would worry that I was unable to sleep. Trying to alleviate that unnecessary fear, I quickly added, "I was just getting myself some juice when I heard the bed creak."

As we walked back to the bed, the same smile that had appeared only minutes before spoke an appreciation with the same silent tones as its first message.

"Would you like something to drink, too?" I offered.

"No, I'm fine," she answered, in the same soft-spoken tone I had heard for nearly fifty years.

I'm fine. This tiny specimen of a female - alias "one of the weaker sex" - had no complaints. She had gone through two blood transfusions, and cancer and reconstructive surgery only days before. Her feet and legs were so swollen that even the expandable Velcro-fastening slippers would not fit her. Bags and stints were still an unnatural part of her. But she was "fine."

Cheree Miller had been fine ever since she met me in that hallway eight days ago as she entered the hospital for the test that would tell the world that her body was housing a horrible enemy. Cheree Miller had been fine all my life whenever I would ask her how she was. Cheree Miller was fine following any illness, or the wreck she had suffered several years back. In all my years, I had never once heard her complain about anything, illness or otherwise. And as I made my way back down the stairs to my vault of memories, I suspected that Cheree Miller had been fine the day she gave birth to me after two days of labor and walking the hospital floors, and delivering a baby that, in today's world of healthcare, would have required a Caesarean section. *And*, Cheree Miller was most assuredly fine even when they told her that the baby she had just severely struggled to bring into the world might not make it, and that the baby's birth had altered her physical being in such a way that she would never reach her dream of having eleven children - enough for an entire ball team.

Appreciating my mother even more as I valued her stamina and attitude of life, I took a quick glance at Daddy in the bedroom across the hall. *Good, he's still asleep*. I couldn't help but wonder if this was the first time that my parents had slept in separate beds since my childhood days when I would get sick and want to sleep in the bed with Mama. Sure that it was, except for nights that Daddy had spent in the hospital after surgeries, and the nights he had sat up with his own father. I closed his door behind me.

As I tiptoed downstairs, I had to hold in sudden laughter as I remembered the last time I slept with my mother. It was sometime during the year after I got a talking doll for Christmas. During the night, I had gotten sick, and Daddy and I traded off beds. Mama tucked me in, turned out the lights and laid down herself just in time to hear a blood-curdling scream from across the hallway. Both of us sat straight up, and she yelled to Daddy to see what was wrong, literally making it to my bedroom in two leaps.

It was a good thing that Mark Miller was not a user of profanity, or I would have gotten a first-rate education of the English language as, in the darkness, he had laid down on top of my doll, and it had cried, "Maaama," in a slow, whining tone.

Close behind Mama's steps, I joined her in hysterical laughter as she practically had to peel Daddy off the ceiling. Of course, he did not think it was too funny at the time, but that did not matter to Mama and me. We would have laughed no matter what. And I learned that the slogan about 'laughter being the best medicine' was right, for I felt immediately better that night.

Laughing again at the same remembrance, I lowered myself back into the world of my own making, in the rocking chair with the two books back in my lap.

No, not my making. The making of Mark and Cheree Miller. I stared around at the blankness of the room, sensing again all the spirits in my midst. *No, not the making of Mark and Cheree Miller. The making of all the generations of my fellow ancestors.*

Looking down at the Bible storybook, I rubbed my fingers across its textured, white-leather cover with its gold engraved letters. The letters had lost none of their shiny, lustrous beauty over the course of years. And the thickness of the leather-bound cover showed the respect of care that had been given to it during its use. Although the book had been read cover to cover many times over, it had been of a vintage when people believed that Bibles and the like were to be displayed on coffee tables and, by token of their very existence, were sacred and holy. Thus, except for the signs of discolor from the age of the white leather, there were no marks of its use.

I remembered the day that the salesman came to the front door with his black suitcase stuffed full of Bibles and related storybooks. Although I went on with my playing at the time, I could picture him sitting in the living room, pulling out his literary wares and displaying them on the wooden coffee table.

He had rated little attention in my four-year-old mind, and it was not until years later that I made the connection that my mother had bought the most expensive Bible storybook that the salesman carried. She would have nothing but the best for her little girl when it came to telling the stories of their background and heritage. A background and heritage that began with the first story in the book, the creation of Adam and Eve.

I opened the book carefully, noting the gold edging of the pages. Reading to myself, I could hear Mama's voice as she read me that first story on the very day she gave me the book. It was after all the fun and excitement of my fifth birthday party.

It was funny how I could still remember all the presents. There was a pretty little Sunday dress, in a plaid of different shades of browns and rusts, with a white cotton collar, from my Grandma Rose, and a swing set that Daddy spent the entire Saturday morning putting together before my little friends arrived for my first real birthday party. I could still see the pin-the-tail-on-the-donkey game, and taste the tri-colored Neapolitan ice cream and the chocolate birthday cake.

My favorite present from a guest had been the little pink plastic purse with little plastic hair bows inside. There had been pink bows with flowers, blue bows with dogs, yellow bows with cats, white bows with lambs, and bows of every color to match every outfit I had. I could even remember thinking how odd it was that the little fat boy with the four eyes, the boy that fit the description of the nerd from every class, gave me such a cool present. Now I knew that it was only because his mother picked it out, and because she, too, had a daughter, so she knew what a little girl would like.

Rubbing the textured cover, I again read from the Bible storybook. The questions at the end of each story caught my attention. As I looked over them, it amazed me that I was able to answer them at the age of five. Some of them were quite difficult and required some thought rather than straight answers. Yet, I could remember Mama sitting with me on her bed, on my bed, or in the living room, reading to me and helping me to understand the truths of each story.

Like the valuable lessons I had first learned from that storybook, so was the lesson I was now learning. It struck me, in the process of surmising the content of the stories and the questions, what a patient person Mama was. Oh sure, I had known that my entire life, for I had never once heard my mother raise her voice to me, or any other person. Nor had I heard her ever voice any damaging statement toward anyone. But besides those factors, she had managed to take a curious five-year-old, a story passed down for many centuries, a question way over a child's head, and blend them all together in not only a reasonable, understandable fashion, but in a way that was fun and that sparked my interest for another story. Some days I begged for as many as five stories.

My recently learned lesson also reiterated the fact of what a godly creature my mother was. She truly did fit the scriptural passage about a virtuous woman that I had read earlier in the day. It was obvious what a wonderful teacher she would have been, and fortunately, I had had her all to myself. Every child should have been so lucky.

Feeling my eyelids drooping more and more by the minute, I decided to put the books back in their places on the shelf, but not without first closely examining the picture of the illustrator's portrayal of Adam and Eve in the garden. What a beautiful garden of Eden they had been given. And what a mess they had made of it.

I laid down thinking of what a beautiful childhood I had been given. And what a mess I had made of some situations I had encountered throughout my life. *How closely their story relates to mine*, I thought, realizing how much their actions must have hurt God, yet how much he still loved them. *Kinda like the way Mama and Daddy have always loved me in spite of my sometimes foolish actions.*

Seven

$\mathcal{M}$y body did not even grumble about the lack of sleep from the night before. The minute I heard Mama move, I was up the stairs, and in the kitchen awaiting her entrance. She had always been an early riser, so I welcomed the fact that she had slept in this morning. It was actually 6:45.

"Good morning, sleepyhead. I thought you were going to make a day of it!" I said, giving her the words that Daddy had always shot at me when I came home from college and attempted to make up for the week's hours of lost sleep.

"Yes, I did stay in bed longer than usual, didn't I?"

"It's alright. You're entitled."

"What time did you finally go to bed last night?"

"I went to sleep right after I looked at a few pages in a book. Slept just like a baby."

The thought hit me that I had slept like a baby, probably because I felt the same security in this house that I had felt in my home as a child.

As I poured Mama's coffee and cream, and scrambled around in an unfamiliar kitchen making her breakfast, I remembered other family members and friends asking if I wasn't upset when they made the move to the mountains.

The thought that ran through my head at that moment was the same answer that struck me each time I had been previously questioned. *They've been caregivers. They deserve this, and I'm happy for them. The house was not my home. My parents' love was my home, and that will be the same wherever they are.*

I had been right in that answer, for even I had just admitted that I had slept like a baby in their house. And as for Daddy, he thought he had died and gone to heaven. "Happy as a pig in mud," Grandma Rose used to say.

Mama's ability to stay awake amazed me, after the gruesome battle she had just undergone. A part of me wondered if it was because, in spite of her strong front, she wanted to savor every moment of life she possibly could.

I cleaned the breakfast dishes and yearned to examine the photo album I had spied the evening before. *Maybe I shouldn't worry about looking at pictures right now. It might make Mama feel a sense of depression, looking at all those years of memories.*

But as the morning wore on, my curiosity got the better of me. Finally, I could stand it no longer.

"I took a journey down memory lane last night in the bookcase downstairs."

"You did?"

Mama looked pleased that I had taken the initiative to look through the shelves. Then her mouth turned down in a changed expression and I knew that she was concerned that perhaps I had been unable to sleep after all.

Before she had a chance to question me, I headed off her misgivings. "Don't go thinking that I was awake on account of you. I slept perfectly fine," which was not a lie. I had merely opted to spend some time making myself sleepy before I tried to lie down, knowing I had been too keyed up to shut my eyes.

It was one thing to have stayed at the hospital with Mama. There was a certain peace knowing that the nurses were only a buzz away. But here, even though it was marked territory, there was a hint of the unknown, a natural worry about what could or would happen if a problem actually occurred.

I opted to change my own line of thought before she hit me with a barrage of questions. But the glow in my mother's face told me that I had no need of worry. She looked like a cherub, totally aloof of any anxieties of my own making.

Mama had always lived by Franklin's adage, "Early to bed, early to rise." I had hated that quality about her when I was a child. But now, anxious to hide in my downstairs retreat with all the relics from my past, I was glad she still adhered to the old saying. I was excited to have several hours to browse through all the books before I called it a night myself.

Even though the scenes in the pictures were from years ago, the memories were so striking that they seemed like they were from only yesterday. Mama and Grandma Rose had carefully organized the photos so that they appeared as chapters in my life. It was most pleasant to have all the pictures take on a life of their own as I flipped from page to page. There was no time lapse in trying to recall the events, and the message that repeatedly rang loud and clear was that I had lived a most wonderful childhood and youth to have the images come back to me so readily and clearly. Not at all like the people who spent their days trying to forget their pasts, or trying to put the pieces back together. It suddenly hit me as to how real and traumatic the problem of troubled childhoods really was, and just how truly blest I had been all my life.

I heard Mama stir in her room, and immediately ran to see about her.

"I'm fine," she whispered, tiptoeing to the bathroom, trying not to wake Daddy.

"Can I get you anything?" I whispered back, amused at the fact that in her weakened condition, she was still trying to be a caregiver for my father by letting him get a good night's sleep.

Expecting a rejection at my offer, she caught me off-guard as she spoke, still in a low voice, "I do think I might like some grape juice."

"Coming right up," I beamed, glad that I could be of service.

As I made my way back from the kitchen with juice in hand, I met Mama teetering down the hall.

"What are you doing up?" I asked, not scolding, but letting her know that there was no use in her expending energy. "Don't you think you should be trying to rest as much as possible during the nights?"

"The nurses told me that it was good for me to walk. I figured if I was going to be awake, I might as well put in a few extra steps."

Her smile and that soft, gentle face with her glistening eyes made it impossible for me to say anything to the contrary.

I walked through the house with her, holding onto her purse, as she lightheartedly called it, making it easier for her to move while giving me a purpose to drag along. Although I was sure Mama *would* be fine, if for no other reason than her sheer positive attitude, I somehow felt my own selfish need for her presence.

The surgery had proven more miraculous than we could have ever hoped, and I knew that this was not going to be the end of the road for Cheree Miller. But I also knew that my mind had gone the way of most others in my present 'boat' as I had already begun to cherish each moment and small memory with my mother.

After getting Mama tucked back in her bed, without arousing so much as even a peek from my father, I hurried back downstairs to the picture album. I seemed drawn to it as if it were a treasure map to some long lost gold, and for all intents and purposes, that is exactly what the album was. For it held long lost memories of a happy time, of the love of a family. Not only of a child and her parents, but of generations of grandparents and cousins, who were like siblings to an only child, and aunts and uncles whom I knew cared for me.

I happened to open the book to my first Easter. There I stood, hovered, looking at something on the ground, my face visible only enough to see a huge tear on my fat, little cheek. Laughing at the short, squatty miniature body in the picture, typical of most toddlers that age, still carrying around their baby fat, I did not have to look to see what was on the ground. It was clearly recognizable in my mind. Not from the actual memory of it, but from the countless times of looking at the fallen object as a child and hearing the story behind it.

On the ground lay a small, ceramic yellow chick that had dropped from my Easter basket. I was not sure if the tear was from fright that I had done something wrong, or that I sensed something was amiss, or if I was truly attracted to the little object and did not like the fact that it was now missing from my basket. The tear brought a laugh as I imagined how much I resembled a mother hen, with one of her eggs missing from her nest. My oversized, ruffled bonnet even resembled the chicken's comb.

Then the reality hit. How current the situation seemed as I, the daughter, now felt like the mother – a mother hen – knowing that something was amiss in my nest. A sigh escaped as I shut my eyes and felt that imaginary tear on my cheek again.

I opened my eyes to examine the picture more closely. The first thing that caught my attention was my dress, with the puffy short sleeves, and the layers of frilly petticoats underneath the skirt, and my little turned-down nylon socks and white patent shoes. Funny, I had no idea what color that dress was that I could distinctly see in the black-and-white photograph, but I remembered vividly the little chick that was hardly visible lying on the ground.

Another item that caught my attention was the

flower garden in the background. There were daffodils in full bloom in patches around the yard at my grandmother's house, the location of the picture. It had been made while my father was still away in service, so my mother and I were living with Grandma Rose until Daddy's return.

The next picture in the album had to have been the next frame on the film at the time, for there knelt my mother beside me, reaching out to comfort me. The next picture, again in consecutive order, amused me, for there I sat on the ground, my short legs giving way to my squatty body until I fell into a sitting position, with everything from the basket scattered on the ground around me. But I was happy with the little yellow chick in one hand, and the other hand shoveling a piece of Easter candy into my mouth, adding to the size of the squatty little body.

Grandma Rose stood in the background of that picture, in front of the flower garden, amused at my ultimate contentment. Three generations of smiles, three generations of love, flanked by a background of natural beauty, casting the Earth Mother's smile to ours.

One page. One page of memories. One page of one day in my life. But one page that told many stories, not only of my lifetime, but of the lifetimes of my mother and grandmother, as well. That page told me that I had learned to walk before I was one year of age, for Easter came before May. It told me that Easter must have been late because the yellow daffodils were already in full bloom. It told me Easter Day of that year had been beautifully sunny and unseasonably warm – a far cry from the cold and rainy day I had been born. And it told me that I had been completely surrounded by love from birth.

I ran my fingers over the photos as if that was going to magically put me in touch with mystical vibrations from the pictures. But I knew it was only a gesture that somehow seemed to hold me in touch with them.

My parents' old house materialized in my thoughts as I remembered the exact spot in the hall closet where that chick sat my entire life until Mama and Daddy moved to this mansion they owned on a hilltop. Again I shut my eyes, recalling the voices of my mother and grandmother singing an old gospel song about a mansion just over the hilltop.

Mama's words from the morning of the surgery tore at my heart. "I'm not afraid, for if it's time for me to go, I know God's got a great big screened porch with a rocking chair waiting for me."

Mixed emotions claimed me as tears made their way down my cheeks while I audibly chuckled. God had deemed that Cheree Miller was going to have to be content with her present mansion on a hilltop. There was one thing that I felt sure would be surrounding that screened porch and rocking chair on that proverbial hilltop – a garden of flowers, all assorted pastel shades of purples, pinks, yellows and blues.

I made myself a mental note to ask Mama about

the whereabouts of that chick the next time I went up-stairs to check on her. As badly as I would have loved to have that chick right now, I knew that it was far more important for my mother to hold onto that material part of our past, for the present. But, no matter where it was housed, it was definitely time for that little yellow chick, knicks and all, to make a reappearance.

As I closed the photo album, I decided that the page of pictures told me one more thing. It told me that the little chick was going to find its way beside Mama's bed before the day was done.

Eight

*E*veryone always looked forward to Aunt Louise's arrival with great anticipation. But today seemed even more exciting than usual. I knew that Mama and she both loved company and old stories, and that Daddy loved her like his own sister, so the three of them were going to have some very memorable days recalling all the tales of their pasts. And on top of that, Doug thought of her as an extra grandmother, so he was ecstatic that he was going to get to spend more time with her than usual.

I had called her the evening before to ask if she might like to go straight to Cheree's instead of her summer home. She was thrilled at the idea. Her final remark ran through my head.

"I'm just afraid that I might be putting you out too much. I know you have to be back in town for Sunday."

That worry brought a smile to my face as I got ready to go to the airport. All the years that she and Mama had run my cousins and me to movies, swimming pools, and shopping centers brought back fond memories as I busied myself until her arrival. Only now did I realize that the time they spent playing taxi driver was their sharing time. It gave them an opportunity to get out from under the tyranny of Grandma Rose's iron-clad rules, and a breather from us kids, knowing we occupied each other.

I laughed, thinking about the pictures I had run across just days ago in Mama's photo albums of me with my two cousins. Aunt Louise, Uncle Edwin and Mama each had a child born within a six-month time span, and we were placed in a playpen to duke it out from the beginning. No wonder we were so used to each other. I guess they figured if we didn't kill each other in the first five years of our lifetimes, we weren't going to.

The sight of those pictures had made me laugh aloud as I keyed in on the expressions of our infant faces. We were all less than a year old, but even at that early age, it was most apparent that we all had our own individual personalities, and that we knew exactly how to get under the skin of our parents. Every single shot had one of us making some sort of crazy face in the camera, as if it were planned by the three of us babies just to get on their nerves. We had all laughed for years about those pictures that Grandma Rose had in the front of her photo album. And then, they were forgotten. That is, until Mama's recent calamity sent us all flinging wildly, as if through the chute leading back into a time tunnel, to long-buried memories.

No, Aunt Louise. This is not a chore for me, but a part of the treatment plan for Mama. A vital part of the treatment plan. I grabbed a light sweater in case the evening mountain air had a chill to it, and headed out the door. *And it is also a part of the healing process for you, too, dear Aunt.*

I knew it was important for my aunt to see her sister, to see that she was okay, and to alleviate a lot of her worries. It had been plain to hear in last night's conversation that Aunt Louise's mind was not on her summer visit, as it usually was, but on her sister's health.

Aunt Louise had been a nurse for years, retiring at a point just before Grandma Rose's massive stroke when she felt she might be needed to help with my grandmother, and then my uncle – her brother, and now my mom. And I knew that she would use those years of skill to make sure that Mama was getting everything she needed.

That same concern was still evident as she exited the plane, with the first words out of her mouth inquiring about Mama's present condition. Being an only child, I was touched by her love and devotion for her sibling, her only living immediate relative, whom she got to see for a couple of months during each year.

We quickly grabbed her luggage, and made our way toward the interstate, going the opposite direction from which we had in all her previous visits. As soon as I made the first turn away from Union County, I sensed the tension in her body and her voice. Thank God, I was going to be able to be there for her when she first saw her sister. It was evident that it was going to be an unwelcome hardship.

I vowed to make the two-hour drive entertaining for both of us. We laughed at the many funny instances we had experienced together over the years, beginning with my first year of existence.

Mama and Grandma Rose had left me with my aunt to go to a funeral. While they were gone, Aunt Louise, being the helpful and caring individual she was, decided to give me a bath. She tried her hardest to get rid of the dab of chocolate in the bend of my elbow, finally scrubbing with all her might, but to no avail. It eventually dawned on her that I had a brown circular birthmark, which was now raw and red from her efforts.

I began to see that our recalling of memories was more than just a laugh, but a settling factor for Aunt Louise as we neared Mama's house. We decided to get dinner at a fast food carry-out so that we could get to Hendersonville sooner. As we approached our destination, I called ahead and left instructions for Doug, who was staying with his grandparents during his summer break, to unlock the door.

Immediately he knew I was up to something. "Is Aunt Louise with you?"

"Yes, but don't you dare tell anyone. We want to see the surprised look on Mama's face."

"You got it. How much longer will you be?" I could hear the mounting excitement in his voice.

"About twenty minutes. Be watching for us so that we don't have to knock."

"Okay, but MaMa doesn't have dinner cooked for you and we have already eaten."

"We stopped and grabbed a sandwich, so we're good to go. Just open the door when we get there."

Doug, like I, knew that Mama would be concerned about being the quintessential hostess, graciously serving a full-course meal to everyone. But I knew that this was her chance to be pampered for a few days, at least as long as Aunt Louise was there, and it might as well start with tonight.

I suspected my call had already gotten a myriad of questions from Daddy, knowing that Louise was expected this afternoon. Doug was a smart guy, on the Dean's list, so I was counting on his creative ingeniousness to distract his grandparents for the next ten minutes.

The look in Mama's face when she looked up from her rocker and saw her sister was worth whatever time was spent going up the mountain. I knew from the moment they laid eyes on each other that this was going to be the most memorable visit of their lives.

Mama was so weak that she was unable to get up, and the initial reaction for Aunt Louise had to have been difficult. But they sat and talked as if there was nothing out of the ordinary about this visit. Neither of them mentioned the recent cancer, or surgery, or anything unpleasant. I was glad that my mother had learned to trust me enough not to even ask about dinner, figuring I had taken care of it.

I could see the happy twosome were off to a great start, and that this household was going to be rocking and rolling – rocking on the porch, and rolling from laughter – for the next couple of weeks. Seeing I had done my deed, I left them to catch up on years of memories.

The lone trek back down the mountain proved to be a part of my own personal healing process. Besides being glad that I had made this effort for both Mama and Aunt Louise, I had sensed the calming effect that it had on me also. As much as I hated leaving, it was a good thing that I had business of my own, for I knew this was going to be a much-needed visit for both of them. As I turned on the radio to occupy the time on my ride home, a smile of gratification spread its way across my face.

It was obvious how therapeutic the two-week visit had been for all of them. Doug was begging me not to come get Aunt Louise, having enjoyed her visit as much as I had as a child. Daddy tried to get her to stay longer, feeling a great sense of relief by her presence. Mama had enjoyed the visit immensely, and her face showed the effect of this age-old form of medicine.

I was glad that I decided to spend the night and visit before I took Aunt Louise to her summer home. Their never-ending storytelling proved to be a real treat. Although I had heard all of the stories numerous times before, the retelling of each one brought a joy unequaled by previous times. I knew that it was not so much the stories as it was the sharing between these two sisters. And the stories displayed love and affection from their parents and grandparents before them. As I listened to them rattle off their fondest remembrances, I, too, was able to join in the healing process.

My family had never been one to shower each other with affection and words of love, but there was never a doubt as to how much we cared about one another. And listening to these two sisters' tales was like hearing them give each other verbal hugs.

They sat on the screened porch, looking out over the mountain, one of the mountains that led to the Great Smokies - the setting for many of their stories and their great ancestry. Aunt Louise had us all howling with laughter as she began the evening of storytelling. I wondered how many times she had told these tales since her arrival, but it did not matter, for now she had a fresh pair of ears, attentive and ready to listen to all the anecdotes, both hidden and obvious, that could be gleaned from her memory bank.

"The maddest Edwin ever got at Cheer," (the nickname the immediate family had called my mom since her birth, but one for which I did not know the origin), "was the time she came home with mountain socks. 'Them blamed ole charity socks,' he called them when he got home to Mama. They were giving out socks to the welfare children who didn't have anything, and Cheer was only in the second grade. Times were mighty hard in the mountains back then, after the depression and all, and there were lots of folks without. We were poor, but still better off than some. Even so, when they came around to Cheer's class giving out the socks to the needy, she raised her hand and took a pair. Boy, was she evermore proud. And then she got on the bus that afternoon flashing those socks around, showing them off to everybody. Edwin was so embarrassed that he couldn't stand it. It was only because he was in high school, and had a girl he liked on the bus, but he was fit to be tied that his sister had a pair of charity socks. But to Cheer, they were only a pair of mountain socks, and she was awfully proud."

"Anyway, Edwin got off the bus first that afternoon, and went flying in the front door of the house, screaming and yelling the whole while. 'Mama, I want you to whip Cheer!'"

"What for?" Mama asked, never looking up from the washboard.

"She got a pair o' them danged ole charity socks and was swinging them around all over the bus," Edwin ranted, making the motions of swinging the socks in mockery.

"By this time, Mama was laughing uncontrollably. She knew the source of Edwin's anger. And she also knew that Cheer didn't know any better."

"Huh, if the truth be known, we were probably as poor as any kid in school, but you'd have never known it from our parents. They taught us to work for what we had, and that no matter how poor we were, we could always do for others." You could literally see the reflections of time in my aunt's eyes.

"So did Mama get a whipping?" I asked, already knowing the answer.

"No!" Aunt Louise laughed, drawing out the

vowel ending. "But much to Edwin's dismay, the story sure got told over and over at the dinner table when Daddy got home from work that evening, and it got better every time with the telling."

Like all family stories! I mused, as I thought what an appropriate name Cheer had been for my mom. She was five years younger than my Aunt Louise and had been nine years younger than Uncle Edwin. For all intents and purposes, she had probably been like a live baby doll for my aunt, and either a cute little darling to my uncle - or a royal pain! - as she had been in the sock incident.

"But I was the worst of the bunch, I reckon," my aunt rattled on. "It was me that was always getting the razor strap. Seems I stayed in trouble. Daddy didn't have to spank us much, but when he did, we sure knew it."

"I don't know why I was the one that had to be the instigator of everything." She paused, drawing a breath, and still, after decades, looking back for an answer to her comment. "Shoot, Edwin had probably already done it, but I was too young to know it, so I missed out on all his bad examples. Then, of course, I got to be the one always having to drag Cheer around with me, so we were forevermore gettin' in trouble for me being a bad influence."

"Course there was one time she was too young to be involved, and I sure got my tail-end whipped. We were still in town at that point, before we moved back to the mountains. Cheer was only in the Cradle Roll at church, so I must have been about six or seven. But I watched that collection plate go around every Sunday. I don't know why I did it, what made that morning any different. I reckon I decided I'd make me a little money that day. But one Sunday as the collection plate was being passed around, I stuck my hand in it when it went by, and took out a handful of money."

"Boy, oh boy, I never got the like of a whuppin' as I did that day."

Amidst laughter causing tears to stream down my cheek, I asked, "Did you ever take anymore money from the collection plate?"

"No!" she howled, as we all sat laughing and shaking our heads.

An Imogene Herdman before her time, remembering the character from one of my favorite books. I made myself a mental note to send Aunt Louise a copy of *The Best Christmas Ever* for the next Christmas. *In a basket with a dollar in it, of course.*

"The first time I was ever left to watch Cheer by myself," she continued, "was the time I tried to feed her red pepper. I don't know why I was such a mean little young'un. I reckon I did all those things just because I could."

"Anyway, Mama was taking the bus downtown to the store for about an hour, and she left me with Cheer. I decided it would be funny to see her face if she got hold of some pepper, so I cut some off a pod and spooned it into her food."

"I don't even remember how Mama found out about it when she got back home, but believe you me, she did, and went straight for the razor strap. It was worse than when Daddy got a hold of it. My legs had whelps that looked like red pepper for a week!"

The stories were rampant, one after another, with Aunt Louise shedding lots of light on their childhoods. I was sure that she was embellishing each tale, the way that folklore gets passed down from generation to generation, and I knew that these were stories that Doug would tell his children and grandchildren someday when he was flipping through the photo albums, showing them their ancestors. One of the things I loved was the dialect that changed from the days of her educated career to the style of the mountain folk, who were known for their stories. I listened, as she continued to amuse me.

"But Cheer deserved it. She deserved every bit of it. She got back at us, and in ways that she never got spanked. Mama and Daddy just thought it was cute, and typical little sister stuff, so they laughed at her antics, while Edwin and I had to suffer the humiliation from them."

"Just like the time I caught head lice. It wasn't like now, when they realize that anyone can catch them. That was considered dirty and trashy, and you sure didn't tell anyone if you had it. Well, I somehow got them, and Mama sent a note to my teacher with Cheer. So what does Cheer do but march her little self proudly into my classroom and announce with great glee, before handing the teacher the note, "My sister couldn't come to school today. She has a louse!"

"Cheer had been so excited to get to be the messenger that she simply couldn't contain herself. The whole class got a great charge out of that. I didn't think it was nearly so funny when I had to go back and face them all. And did Cheer even get so much as a backhand? No siree! Mama and Daddy just laughed and told everyone they knew."

I decided that the stories were not nearly as funny as was the way Aunt Louise told them, nor to imagine her reactions at the time the stories happened.

"What about Uncle Edwin? Did he laugh?"

"Sure, he laughed! He wasn't the one that had to go back to school and face all his friends after having his bratty little sister tell the whole world that he had a louse!"

"Sort of like how you laughed when he got so upset about the charity socks?"

"Yes, but it was funny watching him get so mad."

I laughed now at the humorous rivalry between these siblings. It was a part of life that I had missed out on, being an only child, but one that, as I listened to my aunt's stories, had probably saved my own parents a lot of anguish. But I did imagine that I would one day sit around the Christmas tree and listen to Doug and Rich share their growing-up tales with their offspring, creating the same kind of laughter and commotion. I also realized that it was these roots, these shared experiences, that kept the family close.

"So Cheer's name fit. She actually did bring cheer to the family?"

"Yes, she did," admitted Aunt Louise, as if Grandpa's foresight in nicknaming his youngest child had just dawned on her. But for that matter, I don't think that my mother had ever caught on to that point, either.

Turning from the laughter and moving to a more serious tone, Aunt Louise asked a question that simply came to her in the midst of telling all of her getting-in-trouble tales. "Cheer, did you ever get a whuppin' from Daddy?"

"Only one time. It was the time we played hooky from school," Mama answered, her smile already breaking into a grin.

"Yeah, here we go again, and that was my fault, too," Aunt Louise said, claiming the blame with a small sense of pride.

The raucous laughter started back up, this time with my mother taking center stage, telling on her sister, as I suspected she had done a few times in the past.

"You and that Thompson girl that lived up on the ridge decided to play hooky one day, and you took me with you."

"Oh, yes," chimed in Aunt Louise, jumping back into the story. "We took you with us 'cause we figured you wouldn't get in trouble, and couldn't tell on us if you were with us."

"Well, I didn't tell," Mama piped up, already

134

laughing at what was coming.

"No, some woman saw the bunch of us sitting out eating our lunch and told Mama about it. She was waitin' on the front steps for us when we got home."

"Yeah, and when she didn't spank us right away, I thought we weren't going to get any whuppin'."

"Oh, I knew better than that!" continued Aunt Louise, with all the experience and authority of an older sister. "You could see the fire in her eyes from the road. I knew that only meant she was going to tell Daddy, and then we'd really get a spankin'. But you know, Mama always spanked harder than Daddy."

"Sort of like Mama with the green belt!" I chimed in.

This got even more laughter as I reminded them of what a family tradition the women in my family had started.

"Yeah, we did get that trait honest," admitted Aunt Louise.

"Anyway, Daddy gave me one lick, and he gave you two," finished Mama.

"Did you ever play hooky again?" asked the older sister.

"Nope," smiled Mama, reflecting on the important lesson that that one lick had taught her. "It hurt me so bad that Daddy had to spank me that I was determined never to make him have to do that again. The fact of him having to do that to me hurt a lot worse than that razor strap."

135

"Well, obviously he didn't hit you like he did me. Or like Mama did!"

I could tell that this last comment was not said with a vengeance, but with a realization that she had pushed harder against the establishment than her baby sister. It also told me that there was a high regard of respect for my grandfather, brought by his love for his children.

"Yeah, I guess I was the worst kid of the lot. It sure seems I got to see the razor strap more than the rest of you." There was a reflective pause. "Whatever happened to that old razor strap?"

"I don't know," answered Mama. "The last time I saw it, it was hanging from a nail in Daddy's old shed, right next to some strings of leather britches."

I knew immediately that one of the first items of agenda for my aunt was going to be to find that long piece of thick leather, and move it from its hiding place to a prominent place in the house.

Whoever said that discipline is bad for a child? Here are obviously two children who are very grateful for the fact that someone loved them enough NOT to spare the rod!

I thought about myself, my growing up years, and the many traditions and values that had passed from these two women into my adult life. And I found myself hoping that I had instilled the same kind of love and respect in my own children. Love and respect that began I didn't even know how many, generations ago.

The stories turned from ones where Aunt Louise

and Mama had been the stars to ones that revolved around the experiences they had shared as a part of their rearing. It was amazing to me how they remembered every single detail. I had always been intrigued by Grandma Rose's ability to remember everyone's birthday, and the exact dates and facts surrounding any occurrence.

As I listened to these women, who by statistics were senior citizens, but who, in my mind, were the same as they were thirty years ago, I realized that they had inherited that trait from my grandmother. *What is it they say about the mind being the first thing to go?* I smiled, praying that this incredible memory was one of the things that passed through my veins, more serious than not.

"Do you remember when Les Brown was a senior and drove our school bus?" asked Aunt Louise, as if an entire gallery of her brain had opened up to reveal a whole array of new stories.

"Yes," answered Mama, smiling at what was sure to follow.

"Blanche . . ." She paused here to tell me that Les and Blanche later got married. "Blanche Goodson rode our bus. It's amazing how many times our bus broke down over on Orchard Hill, so Les could go courtin'. Boy, did we have some good times sitting on that bus while they were out under that apple tree on the top of the hill." Aunt Louise stopped for a minute and you could literally see the images of Clayton Hill and the school bus racing through her head. "Do you reckon that old apple tree is still there?"

I knew the list of things to do during my aunt's visit had just expanded. Now we were going to be on a scavenger hunt for an apple tree that had probably long since been cut to the ground.

"I don't know, but it sure was a good climbing tree." Mama startled me with her quick response.

"How do you know that?" Aunt Louise snapped back, having been caught as off-guard as I had been.

"Because Les must have told the younger boys about that hill. The buses continued to break down on the top of that hill for years – all the way through my years in school. As I got older, we got a little braver, and some of us ventured outside the bus. The boys made a habit of sneaking up behind the bus drivers and their girls, and climbing the tree to listen."

"One day after school, a couple of my friends and I decided to try out the tree. We walked up the hill from one of the girl's houses and spent the whole afternoon eating apples and talking about how many bus drivers had sat under that tree."

By now, I was dumbfounded by my quiet little mom's bravery, but I was more intrigued at how the school's administration had never figured out what was going on over on Clayton Hill. "After all those years, why didn't the principal or the bus mechanics ever figure out what was going on?" I interrupted.

"How do you think they got *their* wives?" snickered Aunt Louise.

Mama added to the explanation. "You've got to remember that communities and towns weren't transient like they are nowadays. Back then, principals and teachers were persons who, after college, came back to their hometown schools to make a contribution to the community."

"So of course the principal knew why the bus broke down," my aunt concluded.

At this point, my mind suddenly wandered off in its own little trance. I had visions of déjà vu, but they were really nothing more than the memory of my grandmother sitting on her front porch with Mama and Aunt Louise, and my cousins and me, all sitting on her front porch listening to her while she told tales of her childhood. It was at about this time of the storytelling that she would make a V with her pointer and middle finger and spit snuff juice out in the front yard.

The memory of that habit, which before had seemed totally disgusting, now brought back fond laughter as I imagined my aunt sitting here, spicing up her stories with the same habit. Grandma Rose had such good aim that she could hit a dog all the way across the yard, and with it running. My laughter grew until I was holding my head from the side-splitting howls that were erupting from my mouth. I was sure that Mama and my aunt thought the laughter stemmed from the stories, and I opted not to divulge the source of my merriment. But as I had earlier prayed that I inherited a wonderful trait from my grandmother by way of my mother, I now thanked God that some of her habits didn't make it down the branches of the family tree.

I listened to them continue with whole volumes of additional stories, many of them spinning from experiences in fields – cotton fields, corn fields, potato patches, or several acre gardens on sprawling farms. Whether it was a garden or a field, the same roots of growing things together, of planting and toiling and reaping, were a part of all our backgrounds.

The symbolism was still the same. Just as the seeds were watered and nurtured with the toil of our hands, so were the seeds of our lives watered and nurtured with the toil of our mother's hearts. More than vegetables, flowers and crops had been raised by this family over the generations of time. The most important and necessary crop of all had long been the most profitable and beneficial crop raised by this family - love.

Familiar words came to mind as I watched the two of them, still talking. *Faith, hope and love – and the greatest of these is love. The greatest of these is love. Love.*

As they continued to rehash old times, I raised a song of thanks for these two women, for what they meant to their families.

I knew that it mattered not what happened from here on out. My mother had left me a fortune. An invaluable legacy. A lesson of love. A love that could not be bought. Free love. God's love.

They did not even notice me as I backed away from the porch and went downstairs to find the Bible in the bookcase. There was a certain passage that was calling my name, and I had to read it now.

My thumb raced through the pages looking for the last verse in Proverbs. *Give her a share in the fruit of her hands . . .*

I closed the book, also closing my eyes. *Dear Lord, please let me give my mother even a portion of the fruits she has given me.*

By the time I got up the next morning, the tales were already floating in the air around the coffee pot. The large stoneware mugs from my grandparents' house had been brought out in honor of my aunt's great coffee-drinking reputation.

I helped myself to a plate of bacon and eggs, and moved out to the table on the screened porch. The mountains were especially beautiful this morning. As I glanced down at Mama's rose garden, I noticed how brightly the dewdrops on the roses glistened in the sun.

Suddenly, my visions of the past were joined by sounds of the past, as I imagined my mother singing her favorite hymn in her beautiful, rich alto voice. *I come to the garden alone, while the dew is still on the roses. And the voice I hear ringing in my ear, the Son of God discloses.*

My food no longer held the attraction it had as I had smelled it coming up the stairs. I walked down the steps from the porch leading to the garden, and took a stroll amongst the tall bushes, clothed in full blooms. There truly was a peace that accompanied the lush pastel petals and sweet fragrance of the flowers. I could truly empathize with the sentiments of the poet who had first penned the words of the hymn. No wonder Daddy went to such lengths to keep these roses so beautiful.

I began to wonder about the man who had lived here before my parents. He was an artist whose wife had suffered a long and gruesome illness. As a hobby for himself and something for her to enjoy, he had started this rose garden. His hard work had paid off, not only for his wife, but now for my mother. I found myself wishing I could thank him as I picked one of the pale pink blossoms and carried it back upstairs to Mama.

Returning to my breakfast, the realization hit me as to how painful it was going to be for Aunt Louise to leave Mama. The good thing was that her summer home was my grandparents' old house, so there would be some comfort there. But I hated she did not have a rose garden of her own. At least there would be plenty of camillas, irises and daylilies. I would offer to stay with her, but I knew she would decline.

Oh, well. That will give her some time alone to sort through all of this. I knew that my daily prayer list had increased by one.

Nine

$\mathcal{D}$addy knocked on my door an hour earlier than I had anticipated. As badly as I hated mornings as a rule, it was amazing how bright-eyed I was when I heard the familiar tap. Normally, I would have grunted, moaned and rolled back over, begging for just ten more minutes of sleep. But I knew that I was needed this morning, more for a right hand to my father than for moral support and physical help for my mother. The hour's time difference was no mistake – it was a cry for my presence. And I was glad to oblige.

I let them out at the day surgery, parked the car and found my way to the check-in desk. Just as I rounded the corner to let them know I had joined them, I heard the admitting nurse say, "I need you to sign one more form. Do you have any weapons?"

The laughter bolted from my mouth before I could even think about stopping it. My reaction caught the attention of the only other two persons already congregated in the waiting area, and sparked a giggle from the asking nurse. She could look at my mother and see that even if she had carried a weapon, she was too weak to use it. But the real clincher was, as I explained to the nurse, and the other visitors, "Cheree Miller with a weapon would be more dangerous than the weapon itself."

Even the thought of such was majorly out-of-character for my mom. Yet, as my minister had analyzed the morning of the terrorist attacks on New York and Washington, "Cancer is a terrorist. It causes fear and havoc in one's life, family and household."

Remembering the televisions blaring with news of terrorist attacks on that morning, I now saw that my minister's analogy was correct. The trepidation on Daddy's face told the tale. The lack of expression in

144

Mama's face was the storyteller. Here stood my parents, the pillars of strength that had shaped my life, my very existence, limp and waiting to be told what to do and expect next.

Cancer - a terrorist - infiltrating one's being, taking over one's life . . . No wonder Daddy had expressed such relief on the telephone two evenings ago when I told him I was going to be with him at the hospital. It had been a morning like this six months earlier when he unsuspectingly accompanied my mother to the hospital, only to have had his world blasted by the bodily equivalent of a Tomahawk cruise missile, shattering memories, dreams, ordinary life - everything - until he was crumbled completely to the ground.

A sense of tranquility rippled through every vein of my body as I also recalled the calm that accompanied their reactions six months ago. When attacked by the news of Mama's assaulter, neither of them had flinched in their faith – a faith that ultimately served as the power that had overcome that terrorist. There was no doubt how they would handle today, no matter what the outcome of her colonoscopy.

I focused on Mama's last words to us as they wheeled her back to the surgical suite, "I'm fine. I don't have cancer anymore. They got it all." And then there was her smile.

My mind told me that physically, I did not know what the doctors had done. But I did know what the Great Physician had done. And there was definitely no terrorist in her body.

Daddy and I walked back to the waiting room, and I watched the patients that stepped off the elevator. Each of them went through the same questions that Mama had been asked.

Does this woman, who has to possess some semblance of intelligence to have this job, actually think that someone is going to admit to having a weapon? People who are dumb enough to come in here with something illegal certainly aren't going to tell the world.

My ramblings stopped cold. *Or are they?* My thoughts recounted stories of people who had actually gone into public places, carrying weapons, and announced their entry, proud that they were taking control of a situation through the use of guns and ammunition.

Then it hit me, just as clearly as if someone had struck me with a weapon. I had been completely wrong in my thinking. When Cheree Miller had entered Pardee Hospital six months ago, she *had* been carrying something – *in* her body. But it was a terrorist – *not a weapon.* To many, it would have been a weapon, but not to my mother. It could only be a weapon if she allowed the terror of it to infiltrate her whole being with fear and trepidation. *And she didn't!*

A part of me wanted to go back to the nurse's desk and say, "Excuse me, but my mother, Cheree Miller, *is* carrying a weapon. It's called faith, and it's a lot mightier than even those five pebbles that David slung at Goliath."

I couldn't help but laugh, catching sideways stares from those around me. Suddenly, the image of my mother, tiny little thing that she was - now even smaller since the chemo treatments - coming in here with holsters full of huge guns, all of which were stocked with a plentiful supply of ammunition . . . called faith, became most enlightening.

Yea, verily, Cheree Miller was carrying weapons, and she intended to KICK BUTT!

The visual image was too funny. Yes, it was way off in left field. Yes, it removed the fear of what the doctors might find. And yes, it was a little crude for me to be analyzing the situation in this manner and laughing aloud at my thoughts. But yes, it was, in reality, exactly what was going on with my mother. I wanted to shout out, "You go, Mom!" but my better judgment did at least stop me from going that far.

How many people actually did enter this hospital with a weapon - the most powerful weapon known to man? I also wondered how many of those persons carrying weapons even thought of their defensive power in those terms.

Another nurse stopped my ramblings when she called out, "Miller family," and sent Daddy and me up to Mama's room to wait for the doctor. I glanced back at the desk, and silently thanked the nurse for prompting such an insightful morning.

The surgeon entered Mama's room and reached for Mark's hand. "She did fine." Those same words that were generally the first three out of a surgeon's mouth after any surgery. I had learned over the years that the familiar short phrase was usually followed by a "but," with an expression on the doctor's face that served as a sedative for the remainder of the sentence.

Here stood a doctor who had been entirely jovial and full of smiles on each of the previous occasions I had encountered him following one of my parent's surgeries. Only this time, there was no smile. There was a stern face. A face covered with concern. Concern for the waiting family as much as the patient. A patient who was obviously a martyr, a heroine in the eyes of a waiting spouse. A waiting spouse who was unwilling to hear anything but good news.

It struck me that the role of being the strong arm, the foundation of the family, had just been passed from the mother to the child as I prepared to hold myself erect, feet firmly planted on the floor, so that I could catch my father and protect him from the coming blow, both physically and emotionally.

My gut reaction was to take my father and guide him over to the chair and let him take a seat, but there was no time for that, for I heard the doctor's voice continue, "There are no polyps, but . . ."

Oh, God, there's that word. Please protect my daddy.

". . . we did find two more nodules in the rectum." I glanced at my father's face. His eyes were intent on every word that came out of the doctor's mouth, and I could tell from the gaze on his face that he was listening, yet he was not hearing. "They could very well be scar tissue from the last surgery, and that is what we're hoping for, but we are sending them in for a biopsy report. I'll have the report when you bring Mrs. Miller in for her follow-up visit next Wednesday."

"Thank you," Mark replied.

I could tell from the tone in my father's voice that he had heard "scar tissue," and that was all. Was that all he really heard, or was that all his mind was accepting? His hands were in the grip that they always were when he was intent on a subject. I looked at those hands, clasped together in front of him, with his two forefingers pointed upward and touching. My conscience took over my literalist mind as it occurred to me that perhaps my father was simply following his positive instincts, which relied upon that age-old adage, "Don't make trouble."

Okay, God. I'm going to accept this as the 'Innocent until proven guilty' theory. There is no problem until the report tells us there is a problem.

I looked back at my father's face. I saw in that face that his present attitude about this was the only way

Daddy could handle the news. Sure, my father had me, and two wonderful grandchildren, but we were special attractions, only physically there at certain times. My mother was his life, his helpmate, his chosen one from God.

His hands were beckoning my attention. I looked at him, standing there without an ounce of concern in his face, and stared at those hands. Suddenly, it dawned on me what seemed so odd about those hands. Then as I thought about it, I realized it was not odd at all, but rather, truly insightful. For Mark's hands were in the shape that we all learn in pre-school church finger plays that say, "Here is the church, here is the steeple. Open the door, and here are the people."

My father's hands were in the shape of a church with a steeple! I wondered if he even knew the symbolism in those hands, or if they were simply in a subconscious position. Either way, my fears of his lack of acceptance dissipated into thin air as I realized that Mark Miller had the only *real* handle on the situation.

How foolish of me to think that I would be the one holding Daddy up! It had been God the first time, and it was God now. And Daddy knew that. He had expected me to be just as wise as he was, and to have known that from the beginning. It really *was* my company that he needed more than my moral support.

Are you smiling now, God? I laughed myself, realizing how much pleasure it must give God to see one of his children grow in maturity and wisdom. *Okay, I get the big, fat picture now. Maybe it isn't the end of the world to reach forty and all of a sudden wake up and realize you don't hear quite as well as you used to, and that your eyes aren't as focused as they used to be, or that your joints begin to creak and you move a little slower. The mind wins out over physical ability.*

I looked out the window. A sky that had been completely blue all morning was now overshadowed by a huge black cloud moving in over the hospital. The fall leaves that had been so colorful earlier now appeared a dull, limp brown. I hoped this was not an omen, as I continued to peer into the distance and catch the sight of a lone leaf dropping from a limb.

As it fell lifelessly to the ground, I felt a tremendous pain in my body. Tears became so heavy behind my eyes that my face hurt. An unexplainable, *no - VERY explainable* - void took over my emotional being.

For the first time, I realized how traumatic it would be if all the past treatments, the weeks of enduring chemotherapy were all in vain, and I lost my mother. There was no way I was going to let go of these tears now - not while Daddy could see them. I drove them back from whence they came as I heard movement and voices from down the hallway.

The nurses turned Mama's bed into the room. I kept my place by the window so that my parents could have a moment together. Unaware of whether the doctor had told her anything, I was not sure how they would respond to each other, and I felt they needed each other for the first few minutes.

As I gazed out upon the view in front of me, the cloud turned to a light gray, and was slipping away as quickly and quietly as it had moved in, having only cast a dark shadow over the hospital. The trees were again reflecting the luster given to them by the brilliant sunlight, and the air seemed wonderfully free again, out from under the weight of darkness. I saw a wind come through, causing hundreds of leaves to fall and weave their way in circular patterns to the ground, dancing with all the life they had left. The browning trees paraded their flaming oranges and fiery reds, sparkling like gems in the sky as their branches swayed in the breeze, proclaiming to all the world that they were still full of life.

Once again, I was astounded at God's way of bringing me to terms with everything going on in Mama's situation. For here, as the sky and the wind and the colors in the trees spoke to the spectators watching them, so God spoke to me.

My father's life revolved around my mother, but hers also revolved around him. I had been so concerned with her strength holding him up that I had failed to see his own strength and how it played into the picture. Just as the natural elements had miraculously turned darkness into light, so had her appearance to him. His appearance had to possess the same ability for Mama, for neither of them had spoken a word, but only looked at each other as Daddy stood beside her bed, with his hand resting on her pillow. They were each other's sunshine.

I laughed as a large limb suddenly fell to the ground outside, making enough of a crash to startle me from my reflections and analogies, bringing my attention back to the situation at hand.

Yes, God, I can hear you laughing now. You only wanted to remind me Who was in charge here. I truly DID get the big, fat picture, and how beautiful it was. It really WAS worth a thousand words!

Ten

$\mathcal{T}$his was to be a week of surprises. Mama and Daddy had no idea that they were about to have a house guest for a couple of days, nor a gag gift for Dr. Stallings, much less a celebration. I managed to arrive in the driveway just as the garage door came up and their car began to move backwards. Jumping out of the passenger side of my car, I quickly positioned myself beside the driveway, with my thumb pointing out, in the style of a hitchhiker.

Daddy turned to come out the driveway. He saw

me, and slammed on brakes. Mama's excitement at seeing me showed in her smile.

"When did you get here?" he asked.

"Just this second, literally. As I pulled up to the garage, I saw the other door open, and your car coming out, so I decided to hitch a ride."

"It sure is good to see you." It was clear to see in his face, and hear in his voice, that I was still Daddy's little girl. "What's in the bag?" he questioned, noticing the brown paper grocery bag I had pulled into the car behind me.

"Oh, it's just a little something for Mama to give Dr. Stallings."

That comment attracted Mama's attention as she turned toward the back seat. I reached into the bag and pulled out a gallon jug – the one that Mama had used only last week before her latest colonoscopy. I had filled it with a mixture of lemonade and a green sports drink to give the appearance of the liquid that had originally occupied the container.

My mother broke into laughter, which caused Daddy to slam on brakes again to see what was causing such a commotion from his normally quiet little belle. He, too, burst into laughter as he looked at the jug, complete with a giant green bow on the handle.

Mama had experienced such a struggle on each occasion that she had taken the liquid, to prepare her for surgery, that she had kidded the doctor about having a party and serving him the same concoction as the beverage. Now I was giving her the chance. We were sputtering all the way to the surgeon's office, anxiously awaiting his reaction when my mother handed him the surprise.

She pulled off her role with excellence as she nonchalantly handed the bag to Dr. Stallings and told him that she brought him a late Halloween present. He opened the bag excitedly, pulled out the jug, and howled with the same laughter that had emitted from all of us earlier in the car.

"This stuff really *is* a horror, isn't it?"

"Yes, it is."

We all laughed for a few more minutes, relating to each other what a terribly horrendous time Mama had gone through trying to drink the gallon before each colonoscopy and surgery. It had made her sick every time, yet we began to chuckle at the stories that had actually been nightmares at the time they had happened.

After a few minutes, the doctor picked his folder back up and opened it. "Well, we really *do* have reason for a party today. Your test results came back this morning, and the polyps are scar tissue from the original surgery, exactly what we expected. So you're looking good, and you don't have to come back for another six months."

I could see the disappointment in my mother's face. She had hoped not to come back for a year, like Dr. Stallings' other patients. But at the same time, her wisdom told her not to object, taking every blessing she could get. This surgeon had truly been a messenger from God.

Mama had known it as well as I had, even though we never mentioned it to each other. She smiled her usual smile, without objection, and asked, "May 9th? That is six months from today."

Before the doctor could answer her, I bolted into the conversation. "You can't come that day, Mama. That's my birthday. You've already been in the hospital twice on that day – once, giving birth to me, and once - "

"- giving the doctors a hard time!" Dr. Stallings joked, interrupting our conversation and returning the air to the jovial mood of only minutes ago. "We can add a week or so to the date so that you two can party without the 'go juice'."

Dr. Stallings had managed to get us all laughing again, promising to try to find an agreeable solution for Mama before the next colonoscopy. It was clear to all of us that his comment meant this was a now-routine semi-annual exam.

The doctors agreed that Mama had lost so much weight, and was so dehydrated from the chemotherapy sessions, that she needed a two-week break before the colonoscopy. Luckily for me, her appointments with the surgeon and the oncologist were on two consecutive days, allowing me to be there for both of them.

Now that she had gotten a ray of sunshine from yesterday's test results, my mother was ready to face a second round of chemo treatments. Today marked the halfway point for her. I had made a big deal out of the occasion, hoping that it would be a springboard to keep her spirits up for the next three months.

I dropped her and Daddy off at the oncology center, and rushed back downtown to McFarlen's Bakery, the first place I had discovered when my parents moved here. The counter was full of trays, all bearing tempting delights, as always, proving why this shop was my greatest weakness on Main Street.

One of the sales women appeared from the back, "May I help you?"

"I wish. I'd love to have one of everything!" was my answer, in complete honesty.

"We can take care of that for you."

"Oh, I'm sure you can. And you have done that for me before, when I've brought my youth choir to Mill House Lodge, or done shows that needed bakery props. My students and choir kids love it when I have to come here!"

The baker gave me a warm, appreciative Southern smile.

"What I need today is a layer cake."

She pointed toward the front door, where a variety of cakes lined the shelves. I had already scanned them and did not find one quite like I wanted.

"Do you happen to have any others? What I was hoping to find was something with a bright pink border, and lots of pastel-colored flowers."

"I just finished one in the back with those colors, but it's one of our small cakes. Probably won't do for what you want."

"Actually it sounds perfect. I only need it to serve four people. May I see it?"

The woman disappeared in the back, and came out with a cake that looked exactly like the one I pictured in my mind. It was a miniature version of the ones I had ordered for Mama's birthdays over the years.

"How did I know that you were going to have exactly what I needed?"

She smiled again, gratified that she could be of service. What she did not know was that I had no doubt I would find the perfect cake here. It was for my miracle-mother, and we were having a surprise celebration.

"Do you have enough room to write in the small space on the top?" I asked, expecting a negative answer.

"Sure. What would you like for it to say?"

"I wanted it to say, 'Congratulations, you're halfway through.'"

"No problem! I'll be right back."

Okay, Rosemary. You had no doubt about the cake. Why should you have doubted the writing?

Yes, God, I hear you. It's just that I thought the writing was supposed to be on the wall, NOT the cake! I laughed to myself, carrying the perfect celebration cake out the door.

I quickly drove back to the oncology center, which opened its new facility that day, and carried in the cake, going through the lobby, and straight to the rear of the building in search of my mother's treatment room.

One of the nurses, recognizing me, peeked in the box, asking, "What have you got there?"

"A cake. Today's the halfway mark of Mama's treatments."

Of course, all the nurses had to come and see the cake, adding their wishes of congratulations to my mother. One of the nurses exclaimed, "That makes your present doubly significant."

"What present?" I asked.

Mama proudly pointed to a pink candle sitting on the counter.

"She was our fourth patient to come through our new facility today. We had drawn a number out of a hat this morning for a door prize, and the number was four."

"Well, aren't you special?" I asked, making a big deal out of her surprise. Picking up the candle to examine it, I teased, "Botanical. Pretty fancy, huh?"

I read the label to see that all the pretty plants adorning the candle were a mixture of rose hips, lily, and passion flower. As I held the large, circular pillar in my hand, a warm spirit filled my being with thoughts of Grandma Rose, *the rose of my life*, Mama, *the lily of my valley*, and our love, *the passion of three generations, shared amongst the flowers of many gardens*.

161

A pillar to symbolize my pillars! How perfect.

Mama looked so beautiful seated, leaning back in the chaise. Her smile was so tender, yet so radiant. She loved me, she loved life, and she loved everyone and everything around her. Even in the thin body that rested in the chair, with needles and tubes running into her veins, robbing her of all the energy and strength and natural immunity that her body possessed, she was truly a heavenly creature.

While Mama rested, Doug and I went out to pick up dinner for our celebration. I had ordered lots of vegetables and foods that would hopefully make the next few days of endless treks to the bathroom less difficult. As much as I wanted her to eat and drink and gain lots of weight, she had gotten to the point that she was afraid to eat, dreading all the after-effects.

I couldn't blame her. It was a vicious cycle, out of her control. And doing what was healthy for her only seemed to worsen the other problems. I had watched her color change, her eyes change, and her entire body change over the past six months. But not once had I seen her smile or her spirit change.

My heart did not know whether to break for this

dear loved one, who had never abused the precious gift of life that God had given her, or rejoice in the strength that He had also given her, the inner strength to deal with any opponent that came into her way.

I decided not to ask why, but to be thankful for the latter, realizing that, like all the times she had watched me suffer, with a broken heart of her own, she had watched me grow in strength and wisdom. So this was with her. It amazed me, though, that she, in her minute frame, was still the strongest and wisest person I had ever known.

She was able to finish her cake between trips "down the hall." I didn't get to give her a congratulatory or farewell hug, because she was not able to come out even long enough for me to see her again. For the umpteenth time in the past few weeks, I had to yell my goodbyes to her through the bathroom door. I left Daddy and Doug with her, knowing that she would be well cared for, and that they would pass my hug on to her later.

The decision for Doug to move in with his grandparents had proven to be a good one. Besides being great company for his PaPa, and a most conscientious nurse for his MaMa, it was a great comfort to me for him to be there. After all, had he not been visiting them when Mama first went to the Urgent Care Center, I would never have known about that. But my son had been forewarned to keep me abreast of every little thing that happened to them. So when an incident hit that would have measured on the Richter scale, he convinced his grandfather to call me. Otherwise, I would not have been at the hospital on the infamous Friday when Daddy found out about the malignancy.

Doug had been able to arrange his classes so that he could commute to school, and still take good care of his grandparents. It had proven to be a most rewarding experience for all of them. I could see that my son's youth was good for his MaMa Cheree's stamina. She would eat for him when she wouldn't eat for the rest of us. And every night, Doug sat and read the Bible to his grandparents since her eyes watered so much that she was unable to read any longer. And every night, they prayed their bedtime prayers together. And every night, Doug tucked his grandmother in the bed, as she had done to him so many times in his childhood. And every night, before he turned out the lights, he would sing her a song, *In the Garden.*

Eleven

$\mathcal{T}$he day finally came when I decided Mama had progressed enough to take a short road trip. It had been amazing that she had been able to attend Rich's high school graduation, but that had happened the week before the chemo treatments started. And like any good grandmother, she had already made up her mind that she was going to watch her grandson walk across that stage, shake hands with the principal, get his diploma, and turn that tassel - no matter what the doctor said.

I had watched the chemotherapy take its toll on her. She had done incredibly well with her treatments. She had not lost any hair, and she was sick only a couple of times, but she had lost way too much weight – nearly a quarter of her body's already small size. The tears that continually dripped from her eyes had slowed enough that she did not have to wipe them constantly. And she seemed to have a little more stamina than most chemo patients.

Of course, it was hard to tell about the last point, for she never complained, and she not once mentioned that she was not as strong as before. I had seen the frustration of the endless trips to the bathroom take their toll, in ways besides the loss of weight. But I knew that I was not about to keep her from doing the things that she wanted to do, for I knew that basic need of 'being needed' was a composite of the healing process. Some days I felt like she was pushing too hard, but she never admitted it, and I had long since learned that at her age, she had earned the privilege of doing whatever her little heart so desired.

Yes, Cheree's system had reached the point that a short trip and a couple of days away were just what the doctor ordered.

Doctor Rosemary, that is!

x x x
x x x
x

The next morning, I jumped out of bed at four o'clock. *How did Mom do it all these years?* I mused, recalling how she had always gotten up at that hour until the cancer surgery.

As I busied myself in the kitchen baking home-made biscuits, cooking ham, and making potato salad and deviled eggs - the same picnic lunch that Mama had packed when we traveled during my years at home - I remembered fondly how much she had always enjoyed picnics.

The thought, of all the Sundays we left after church to go to the mountains or a nearby lake for an afternoon of family fun, brought a warm smile to my face. How many times had I walked the trails or played on the rides at Freedom Park while Mama laid out a lunch under a nearby shelter? And all of those trips were accompanied by a visit to the neighboring Nature Museum by an after-lunch walk through trees. Thinking back, it seemed there was hardly a Sunday during the summers that we didn't go somewhere.

My heart beat even faster at the idea of surprising Mama with my little scheme. As I whipped up the banana pudding for dessert, I realized how important those days of stopping to smell the roses had been to my whole development process and how I longed to have those times again. I made a vow that family picnics were going to become a regular part of my agenda. The boys would still enjoy them. They loved being outside and playing ball.

The art of family togetherness is back in style at the Ellis house. Another of Doctor Rosemary's orders!

By the time Mama was up and dressed, I had the picnic basket and a cooler packed.

"Good morning, Mom," I chirped, giving her a peck on the cheek. "Ready for your mystery trip?"

"I wouldn't miss it."

Another smile spread across my face. Mama had always been up for a trip. It mattered not where I wanted to go, she was ready and more than willing to go with me. The cheerful expression on her face made me question whether she, too, was thinking of how fortunate we were that, through thick and thin, we had managed to remain not only the best of friends, but also wonderful companions for each other. Being a mother with teenagers of my own, I wondered whether Mama had tagged along all those years just to keep from worrying about my whereabouts and what I was doing. But my better judgment told me that was an idle thought, for we had truly enjoyed each other's company, just as I did that of my own sons.

No matter where I was going or what I was doing, Mama had always given me enough rope to make mistakes along the way - to even hang myself - if I made the choice to be that stupid. But luckily, I followed the example set by my mother and, for the most part, stayed on the straight and narrow path.

I couldn't help but recall the day shortly after her return from the hospital when I was sitting out in the garden, going through the mail. The gentle breeze, yet the strong power. An influence that encouraged me to make the right decisions even when I was out on my own.

Yes, my mother IS much like the Holy Spirit. Looking back, I wished that I had possessed the foresight that she had in child-rearing. *Ha! In everything, for that matter.* I shook my head, placing the basket and cooler in the car.

The two-hour trip was filled with wonderful conversation, all of it taking a mother and daughter down treasured paths of memory lane. I wept with tears of joy inside as I heard Mama laugh more heartily than she had during all our time together during the past few years. My original concern that the trip might prove too exhausting for her was erased as I heard the sparkle in her voice and saw the glimmer in her eye.

Turning onto the road that led to both of my grandmother's houses, I knew Mama had figured out where we were going, but in her inimitable style, she never admitted having a clue, not wanting to spoil a daughter's well-planned surprise. Up until that point, we had been on a main road that could have led to the beach, or our favorite lake, or a mountain getaway. The turn was a pretty surefire giveaway as to the destination of our journey.

I wondered whether it might be an emotional event for Mama, but true to form, her face never gave any hint of change in expression. It was clear that she was on a natural high, and she had no intention of losing it, for *any* reason.

She opened the car door and stepped out when we got to her own parents' home place without any kind of spoken invitation. Mama breathed the air in slowly, letting it run its course through her body as if it were one of the chemotherapy treatments. As I stood there, watching her reaction to the environment, I realized that this was the best dose of medicine she had gotten during this whole episode.

This was not the spot I had intended for our picnic, but I realized that a Greater Power had a better plan.

"Mama, why don't we have lunch here?"

The look on Mama's face gave away her unspoken response. I knew that if my mother had been a crier, this moment would have brought tears. And it still might have been so, if her tear ducts had not watered so much lately from the treatments. I retrieved the basket and cooler out of the trunk and made my way over to the huge picnic table that my grandfather had made decades ago, glad that I had remembered to grab a tablecloth at the last minute.

How many tomato sandwiches and watermelons have

I eaten sitting right here in this very spot? I pondered as I proceeded to pull my mother's favorites from the basket and cooler.

"When did you ever have time to do all of this?" Mama asked, as much surprised that I had not only taken the time to fix a picnic lunch from scratch, but that I remembered the entire outdoor menu from my childhood.

"Well, that habit you had of getting up with the chickens does have its advantages. And how could I ever forget all those wonderful picnics we shared all over the country?" I watched the expression on Mama's face, uttering all the thank-you's that I could ever want to hear. "I know. You just can't believe that I can actually make biscuits from scratch, or that I would even *consider* peeling potatoes. Well, just you wait until you see the banana pudding I made for us. I really outdid myself with the meringue!"

I looked closely at my mother. Some people were full of gushy emotions. Cheree Miller had never been that type. In fact, I could hardly remember many times that my mother had actually hugged or kissed me. But the times that she showered me with deepest affection had been many. Now was one of those times.

As we stood there, I couldn't help but place an arm around my mother's petite shoulders. "I love you, Mama."

"I love you, too," were the words I heard in her reply.

There was no feeble voice of a person who had

undergone three surgeries, or a blood transfusion, or six months of treatment for a malignancy that would hopefully never make its way back. Rather, there were inflections of a bright spirit of a woman who had nurtured much love throughout her lifetime, and as was her habit, they came more from the words that she didn't speak than the ones she did.

I thought about all the lessons I had learned from this woman along the way, yet the many differences in the way our bodies and temperaments had been carved out by our Maker. But when it really came down to it, there were far more similarities than there were differences.

In the quietness of this moment, I realized that the quality I cherished more about my mother than any other was the very one that I had oftentimes misperceived as indifference. What a rare gift this ability to keep one's mouth shut really was.

I knew that it was not my nature to be so silent, but over the years I had learned how much I truly did appreciate the times of solitude, when I could manage to find them. And I vowed to take up this quality and carry it along with all the other traits of my mother.

My thoughts turned to my maternal grandmother, who had been my namesake, and Aunt Louise, the only living aunt that I had. This aunt and the grandmother, "Grandma Rose" to all her grandchildren, had been like enemies all throughout their lives together. Yet, when Grandma Rose died, Aunt Louise suddenly took on all the qualities that she had complained about over the years. Qualities that, when it was too late, the aunt realized were not faults, but precious gifts.

Now, here I stood, a grown woman, exuberant in the fact that I had learned what made my mother most uniquely special before it was too late. Although I knew this was not the time for it, I made a mental note to have this conversation with Mama before the day was over, when I could look into her eyes as I thanked her for the most cherished gift she could have bestowed on a daughter. And in my mother's own fashion, it had not cost her a dime!

Of course, the wise mother had taught her offspring the lesson of frugality long ago, and it was one that had now been passed on to my children. I wondered how many generations that trait had passed through before it got to me. Obviously many, for it was so firmly entrenched in all my relatives.

Neither of us could remember a tastier lunch, as our clean plates testified, or a more rewarding time. Even though we were alone here, the spirits of all who had shared food at this table were with us in memory.

Many years were relived during that lunch and early afternoon's hours. I thought back to how many hundreds of tomatoes I had seen laid on that table to ripen, or how many gallons of apples had been placed there in the sun to dry for hand-sized fried apple pies, or Grandma Rose's famous stack pies? Or how many watermelons I had watched my grandfather slice for the entire family, or how many freezers of ice cream he had proudly pulled the towel off as he spooned the treat into bowls?

Far too many to count, I mused, as I began to re-pack the picnic basket and the cooler.

I went to the front porch and wiped off the glider so that we could sit and watch the traffic as we visited for a few more minutes in this sentimental surrounding. A couple of tiny brown spotted toads hopped out from the holes in the bricks supporting the front steps. I couldn't help but snicker.

"Mama, do you realize that three generations have played with those little frogs? I wonder what the life expectancy is for a hoppy-toad, and if generations of toads have lived here like assumed critters of the house?"

The look on my mother's face told me that she was quietly amused, not so much by the small creatures, but by my perception of how this toad family had hung around like the humans that had laid claim on this prop-erty. As I appreciated the lightheartedness of the mo-ment myself, a childhood memory came tearing out of nowhere, grasping my attention and demanding to be shared.

"Please tell me that those were not the cause of Grandma Rose getting down in the front yard, *in a dress*, and showing all us grandkids how to play Patent Sole Leather."

"Sorry. I can't do that," chuckled Mama.

"I was afraid of that. I remember the whole thing

now. We were sitting on the front steps one summer afternoon while all of you women sat on the porch in these very same metal lawn chairs. Grandma got tired of watching us poke sticks at the little baby toads, and decided to see if we could do some ridiculous-looking exercise without hitting our own behinds on the ground." Mama was laughing aloud by this point, so I continued, remembering the power of the best medicine. "She hopped out of her chair, plopped down on her all-fours with her hands behind her, and began to do something that looked like the crab walk except she raised a hand and hit one side of her rear-end with each step. Nothing would do except all seven of us grandchildren were on the ground with her, all making a spectacle of ourselves in the front yard."

Mama was in a full-fledged fit of laughter by now, and I was nowhere near ready to let her stop.

"Now I know why all the cars that passed always blew the horn. I used to think it was just because this is a down-home small community, and that Grandma and Grandpa were so well thought of, but now I know the real truth. They must have thought we would all come out a do a song and dance for ourselves if they blew loud enough. This must have been the local family hot spot for entertainment. You know, sort of like the guy who used to ride my bus that we threw pennies to when he whistled."

"Please tell me you did not do that," Mama reprimanded, with a smile still on her face, like it would do any good all these years later.

"No, of course *I* didn't. I would *never* have done anything like that." When I heard a sigh of relief escape from my mother's lips, I added, "You taught me never to waste even a penny!"

Mama shook her head with her lips pursed, unsuccessfully trying to exhibit a look of disapproval at my comment.

I decided to milk the subject for all it was worth. "You know something? That guy could whistle anything! Why, now they even have some guy who travels around the country whistling the National Anthem at sports events. We heard him once at the Hornets' game. I should look up the guy from school. I'll bet he could make a fortune!"

Mama looked at me, her eyes searching for an answer to her suspicion that I was probably going to find that guy and call to say hello, just to make his day after all these years. My mother knew me very well.

"Mama, you know something. I never did try to intentionally hurt anyone. You and Daddy were wonderful examples of living out the Golden Rule. I must have inherited that from you because I don't remember that value being an effort."

"That's why you got the Citizenship Award when you were in the seventh grade. It was the first time a seventh grader ever received it. Do you remember that night?"

"I sure do. It was a Thursday evening. I was one

of the marshals for the graduating class. One of the eighth graders always received that award, but that year they called out my name. There was a thunderous applause as I slowly rose and moved forward, realizing what an honor that was. I made my way up the steps and across the old wooden stage, and all I could think about was how proud I hoped you and Daddy were."

"We truly were. Your dad was beaming all over."

"Do you know what the greatest thing about that award was?" I asked, suddenly overwhelmed all over again that I had been granted that honor.

"What?"

"When I graduated from the eighth grade the following year, the principal announced they were not going to give the Citizenship Award that year because I would have won it two years in a row. That had never happened before the in entire history of the school." I felt my voice trailing off, in a reflective world of its own.

"Yes, I remember that, too," Mama replied, still beaming with pride.

"Can you believe that out of all the awards and honors I have received over the years, I still count that as being the most meaningful to me? The certificate and the pin still hold a prominent place in my heart."

"Yes, I can believe that. It's just your nature to be the most impressed by the simple things in life."

There was a short silence as we both retraced our steps back three decades, each displaying a quiet, yet pleasant smile on our faces. It was me who broke the silence, of course, not yet having mastered her trait. "Mama, after all these years, I just had a strange thought."

"What's that, dear?" my wise mother questioned, still partially lost in her own thoughts.

"You went to high school at the same place I went to elementary school, didn't you?"

"I sure did. At that point in time, all the grades went to one school. The twelfth grade had been added by then, so I graduated there."

"And that means that's where you addressed your graduating class?"

"Well, not exactly," Mama smiled. I noticed a look of humble pride that I even recollected the story that she had been the valedictorian.

"You never talked much about that, Mom. If it had not been for Grandma Rose having the newspaper clipping in a scrapbook, I would have never known about it. Being the valedictorian is something for which you should have been very proud."

"It *was* something that I was proud of, but I never talked much about anything." Mama muffled a light laugh. "I guess I had been taught not to brag."

"So, if you were always so quiet, how did you ever get up in front of a filled auditorium and make a speech?"

"That's just the point. I *didn't* actually make a speech."

"What?" I asked, more of an exclamation than a

question.

"The principal and faculty decided that the vale-dictorian and the salutatorian did not have to make a speech that year, so we didn't object."

"Why? What happened?"

"I guess they figured I could make the grades, but not the speech, which suited me just fine!"

Mama grinned, and I knew that was all the answer there was. Even then, the teachers had respected my mother's quiet, yet condescending nature. I felt even more of a pride, knowing that we had both broken a record, of sorts, on that old wooden stage.

I delved deeper into the childhood memories of my mother. It had dawned on me, as we sat there talking, that I had never known her to brag about anything. She had always been a modest person, not only in her personal behavior, but in every aspect of her life.

As I thought back, I could not remember a time that she had even mentioned any of her accomplishments. All I had learned about being a good person had come directly from my mother. All I had learned about my mother had come from someone or something else.

My admiration for this woman beside me rose immeasurably as I realized another of the most important lessons my mother had ever taught me. *And what a genius you are, Rosemary. It only took you forty-seven years to learn it!* The slogan about how smart parents became during a teen's years took on a new meaning for me. My adolescence had been relatively painless, looking back on it, but at the time, I must have been like every other teenager, and thought how dumb my parents were. And then, once I got out on my own, I, like all those other teens, was amazed at how smart my parents had become. And then, somewhere in my thirties, it dawned on me just how stupid I had been during all those teenage years, and how incredibly smart they had been my entire life. And now, at forty-something, I was getting the greatest education of my life in the discovery that my mother had taught me more in what she had *not* said than in all the words she had ever uttered. How I truly *did* appreciate her silence!

I looked at Mama. She appeared so frail. She had always been small, but now her frame appeared so tiny that it looked as if I could have put my hands all the way around her waist. Her smile was still there, continuing to give her a most hearty appearance. All the weight I had worked so hard to put back on her during the past few weeks had already disappeared with her last round of chemotherapy.

"Mom, I hate to be the bearer of bad news, but the Fat Farm is back in session! We are going to get you back up to your normal weight." Mama had always been observant of her size and eaten small portions to keep her weight under control. But now she did not even balk about gaining weight, or even adding a few extra pounds. Getting no argument, I decided to push the issue. "In fact, we're going to make you plumb fat!"

She laughed at the thought. "Let's not go quite

that far."

"Okay, you won't have to be fat. But I refuse to settle for less than pleasantly plump."

The next stop on the itinerary was the Miller family cemetery, only minutes away. Even though the mood was far removed from the place we had just been, Mama, again, needed no prompting as she got out of the car and headed toward the plots of her in-laws. Many of her own aunts and uncles from this community were also laid to rest in this cemetery.

We walked from tombstone to tombstone, in silence at first, each not wanting to interrupt the other's nostalgic wanderings. I had originally wondered if this stop might be a mistake in the wake of all that had happened so recently to Mama. The solemn mood of the moment changed within minutes, though, as we were soon in festive conversation about the friends and relatives buried here.

"Mama, do you remember that story of your brother seeing a ghost here when he was about fourteen?"

She broke out in laughter, reminding me of Aunt Louise getting reared up to tell a good one. "Boy, do I.

He came flying in the front door, letting the screen door slam behind him, a stunt in itself worth a good whipping from Mama on any given day. But on that particular day, she had a few of the neighbors over to eat supper, with the new preacher and his wife as the guests of honor. Here comes Edwin, who was supposed to be playing at a friend's house until all the grown-ups left, screaming at the top of his lungs, the dogs yelping to high heavens, paying no attention that the house was full of company."

"Before the door even had time to slam shut behind him, he was yelling, 'Mama, Daddy. I just saw a ghost in the Miller Cemetery. I told you that old graveyard was haunted!' Mama or Daddy neither one got a chance to shut him up, 'cause he was so wound up. He had run all the way home, and back then, we lived a good four miles from the cemetery."

"Everyone was just sitting there staring at Edwin, wondering whether he really had seen a ghost or had simply had the living daylights scared out of him by some older boys hanging out behind the back fence. They'd all heard the tales about the cemetery, and like now, a lot of people figured that souls roamed around loose in the graveyards at night, especially out in the country under all these big old oak trees."

"Anyway, Mama started yelling at Daddy, while her older brother, Edwin's namesake, was yelling at her. 'Mercy sakes,' he shouted, 'can't you do something with that boy? What was he doing wandering through that old place anyways?'"

"Daddy finally got hold of Edwin and took him out the back door just as quickly as he had come in the front, and kept on gettin' it until they were behind the outhouse. I didn't see nor hear anymore out of my brother that evening, but the next morning, I heard Mama warning him not to ever say another word about the whole incident 'cause 'she didn't want him scaring his sisters.'"

I think she was more concerned about her own self, and the neighbors, than she was Louise and me. Of course, Louise wasn't there to hear the whole escapade, and I guess they thought I was too little to know any better. I was just a young'un, and the only reason I got to stay home was because Louise had fed me hot pepper the week before when Mama left me alone with her for a few minutes.

Okay, here's Mama's version of the secret behind the pod of hot pepper for the flowers! "Tell me what happened," I urged, wanting to hear the story from her, even though I had just recently heard it from Aunt Louise.

"Well, Mama was going to take some food down to one of the ailing neighbors." Her words rattled on to tell of an older sister trying to pull a fast one on her younger sibling, while I wondered why all family stories started with the word, "well."

By the time Mama finished her tale, we had walked around the entire cemetery, and rehashed all the memories we cared to about that spot, so we headed back toward the car.

"You do know that your father and I don't want to be buried here, don't you?"

I looked at her, wishing that was the one subject she had not broached. "Yes, I do recall Daddy saying that at some point." I had always wondered why, but I figured it was a question better left unasked.

"Mark decided that a long time ago."

I could tell there was another story somewhere within those words, but Mama was not ready to divulge its details as of yet, so I kept walking. Maybe like Daddy had been with her that first day at the hospital, she didn't know the whole story. But I knew better than to prod.

Some stories are better left untold, I mused, thinking of all the tales buried here, with their owners.

x x x
 x x x
   x

There was one last place of interest on the day's

agenda as I headed the car in the direction of Daddy's home place. It wasn't even a mile away, so there was no question in Mama's mind as to where the next stop would be. As the chauffeur for the day, I slowly rounded the curve to allow the farm to come into view little by little.

Much to our astonishment, a "For Sale" sign hung at the driveway. It was obvious that the property had been on the market for some while, for the grass and weeds were taking over the sign's post, and the sign was hanging down on one side. The fact that no one was caring for the property was apparent way before we got up the long driveway to the house.

None of the flowerbeds were even visible. They had long since been choked out by all the high weeds. Several of the old lap-siding boards on the house's exterior were hanging loose. Even the driveway was so grown up that I had to make my path up it from long-lost memories of my father weaving up it.

"Watch out for the well," Mama warned, knowing that somewhere up the drive there had stood a wooden well, and that cars had to cut sharply to miss it.

"How well I remember the well!" I laughed, suddenly remembering something that I had completely forgotten from years ago. "Don't you recall the time Daddy's brother backed our brand new car into the well?"

Mama now joined the laughter. "Oh, yes! Your father had only bought the car the afternoon before. Mark had fallen in love with that car the minute he saw the first '65 models hit the showroom floor. You know how they say new cars are the only thing that can catch a man's attention faster than a pretty girl," she said, chuckling even harder. "Well, Mark had seen this car in a light aqua color, a new color that year, and decided he would have one before the year ended. It was the year he gave up the season tickets for ice hockey and basketball games so that he could save his money for that car. I guess that's when I knew how badly he wanted it."

"As it happened, we were driving through town the day before Mark's birthday, and he saw his dream car on the parking lot of the local dealership. That was all she wrote. He wheeled into the lot, we took a test drive, and within an hour, we were on our way home in an aqua-colored sporty new car."

I then began to tell my side of the story. "Yeah, that was the day I learned that 'money talks!' That was the first time I was old enough to remember Daddy dickering with a car salesman - back in the 'good old days' before you had to go through an army of people to agree on a price. That salesman could see the look of a buyer in Daddy's eyes, but Daddy refused to pay one more penny than he wanted for that car."

My words stopped as I gave a sideways sneer to Mama. "Wonder where he got that from?" I shot, as she blushed proudly. "Anyway, the guy would take Daddy's offer in the building. The owner kept sending back a counter. Now mind you all this was going on without a single piece of paper or a pencil."

Just then, I felt a giant flash of lightning go off in

my head. "No wonder they could sell cars cheaper back then. They didn't have to buy all the office supplies, or pay so many employees!"

"You're right!" Mama giggled, gleefully amused at my humorous, yet truthful, realization.

I parked the car right beside the house and walked the few steps back to where the well stood. The bucket with the gourd sipper was no longer tied to the rope, and the rope was worn and rotten from years of weather.

The morning glories were fully open and flaunting their blooms, even though it was in the afternoon of a late fall day, as if they had waited to give Mama her own parade of color. Already, memories were pouring out, like someone tossing file folders out of a cabinet, or rather, like the pages flying across the computer screen being saved into another folder.

It dawned on me that it had been over two decades since I had stepped foot on this property. But the minute I got out of the car, pictures took shape, and instead of the overgrown land all around me, I saw the farm as it had been in my grandfather's heydey, *or should I say my heydey?* I smiled with fond thoughts.

Even though it had been years since anyone had planted crops here, I could still envision the huge cornfields where I used to play hide-and-seek with my cousins on weekend visits. I could remember standing on the back steps with the girl cousins, playing school by advancing from one grade to another by guessing which hand the oldest cousin had the rock in behind her back. While we stayed close to the house, the boys all got to hike through the woods, and go fishing in the big pond. I could also recall thinking how sexist that was back then. I wondered what the modern day generation would do if we still got together here for family reunions.

Ah, family reunions!

"Mama, how many people do you think used to come to the family reunions?"

She looked at me as if I had just asked for the solution to some difficult algebraic equation. But considering how many people were in Daddy's family, she could have been right.

"Let's see." I could visually see the calculator in her mind working as she began to name off all the aunts and uncles, and the offspring from each branch of the family, and then the children of their children. "There were a few years when we actually had five generations here at one time. With nine children, multiplied by their children, grandchildren, and great-grandchildren, I think you could safely say that there were at least a hundred people here on any given year. And that doesn't include the years that they invited the siblings of your Grandpa and Grandma Miller."

"That's okay. I get the big fat picture. No wonder there were tables of food that covered the entire front yard. I can still see those tables, made from sawhorses and long pieces of plywood, piled high with all kinds of foods. Even though everyone brought a well-filled basket of food, it was that big old tin tub of lemonade, and the cakes piled high from so many layers, that I remember best."

I made a path out across the front yard, pulling up weeds as I went. "That's where they put the lemonade," I pointed, "right at the end of the table next to that huge oak tree." The tree was still standing, commanding the focus of the yard. "And that's the branch that held the tire swing where all the little kids played," I added, pointing up to the opposite side of the tree from where the food tables had been.

Mama said not a word, but watched me go from one spot to another, like a kid running from aisle to aisle in a toy store, unable to make up his mind what to play with first.

"Do you know I can still taste the coconut and pineapple cakes, and the cream-cheese frosting topped with M&M's she made for all the grandchildren? How many years has it been?"

"Your grandmother could make some desserts. She was known far and wide for her baking. I've never seen the like of the wonderful pies and cakes she would set out at those family gatherings. Why, she used to spend three days baking before the reunion!"

"Yeah, she was good, but Grandma Rose still made the best biscuits."

"I wonder how many biscuits your grandmothers baked during their lifetimes," Mama wondered aloud. "Did you know that my mother got up and made seventy-four biscuits every morning before breakfast until she got married?"

"Seventy-four biscuits?" I gasped, trying to catch my breath at the thought of such a grueling task. "No wonder she got married so young. I'd have been tired of making all those biscuits every morning, too!" Mama laughed at my humorous viewpoint. "How in the world could anybody have eaten seventy-four biscuits at a time?"

"Any *body* didn't. But you've got to remember that there were eleven brothers and sisters in that family, and that they farmed the whole side of a mountain. Back in those days, they worked off all the calories, and bread was a staple at every meal. They made enough each morning to last the day."

"Seventy-four biscuits, though? Can you imagine what I'd look like if you had fed me biscuits at every meal?"

"Can you imagine pulling a plow behind a mule, or picking field corn or slopping hogs all day long?"

"No." I took a piece of grass and put it between my thumbs, making a whistle like I had done as a child. "It's a different day and age isn't it, Mama?"

"It sure is. I've seen a lot of changes in my lifetime, but can you imagine living through what all your grandparents saw? They were alive during both World Wars, the Korean War, the Viet Nam War, and all the other military skirmishes we found ourselves in. They watched the progress of the car, the television set, computers, man's first step on the moon."

"No wonder they were all so smart."

"Yeah, but do you know what their favorite invention was?"

"No, what?" I thought back over the century that had been spanned by my grandparents. My mind could not even begin to fathom all the inventions that had made the scene during their lifetimes.

"Indoor plumbing," she said with a smile. " I remember the day my parents finished their bathroom. They thought they had hit the big time. Mama said she was going to throw her chamber pot as far as she could." My mother laughed again. "But I guess it wasn't as easy to part with as she thought it would be. I found it in their shed when we were cleaning up after she died."

"I guess it was a souvenir of the past."

"Yeah, I guess so." Now it was Mama's turn to be the one lost in another time zone.

I had brought along one last surprise for the day, and this seemed like the appropriate time to bring it out. "Wait until you see what else I have for you." I rushed to the car and pulled out one of the photo albums I had found in Mama's bookcase. "I thought it might be fun to look at these today since we had returned to our old stomping grounds." Handing Mama the book, I went back to the car and retrieved two folding yard chairs. "I thought these might come in handy, too."

Mama smiled, appreciative of all the things I had done to make this day so special for her. It was too bad I had not brought a camera, for it was definitely one of those moments that should have been captured for the book.

And I felt proud that I had shown her the fruits of all her labors through my actions of the day. I truly had left no stone unturned in trying to make this day perfect.

We flipped through the pages, stopping to look at every picture. There was not a lot of conversation as we reviewed the days of our lives, and those who had helped to shape them.

However, Mama couldn't help but laugh aloud when she turned a page and saw a picture of me with a cow, standing in the pasture just behind where we were sitting. I began to laugh, too, more at her than the picture. It was one of those moments that got funnier as time passed.

Mama's face was covered in tears, but not from the laughter. They were a part of the residue from the chemo treatments still playing havoc with her system. But they did not bother her at all. She was so engrossed in the pictures that she seemed unaware that they were even there.

I looked back down at the picture that was giving her so much pleasure, and stared at the big eyes on that cow, and Grandma Miller's old gardening bonnet that we had put on the cow's head.

Buttercup. Ah, Buttercup.

I remembered when Grandpa Miller had bought

that bull. Most of the grandchildren were there one Saturday night, eating popcorn and working a puzzle in front of the fire while all the grown-ups watched The Lawrence Welk Show.

Grandpa took all of us grandkids out back to see the newest member of his lifestock family, and told us that we could decide the bull's name. It just so happened that there were more girls there that evening than boys, so the name "Buttercup" won out over "Mickey" - after the ball player, not the mouse!

"Mama, did I ever tell you the story about how Buttercup got his name?"

"No," Mama answered by a slight turn of the head.

"Well, it was Grandpa's fault. He's the one who had the bright idea to let the grandchildren name that bull, and he should have known better, with that many granddaughters! Anyway, do you remember how I wanted to name everything? To me, living things always held a special significance, just like when I named all of our petunias after my music teachers. Since I was the one with the big imagination, it was my idea that since Grandma Miller liked her flowers so much, we should name things at their house after her flowers. The boys all grunted, but the girls liked the idea. I don't know who yelled out the name "Buttercup," but that was the girls' suggestion. Since there were more girls there than boys, it was a sure-fire given that poor bull was going to be called Buttercup. And since Grandpa had told us grandkids that we could choose the name, he had no choice but to be stuck with a bull named Buttercup. Of course, you will recall that Grandpa called the bull "BC" for short!"

There was a slight smile on Mama's face. I was not sure whether it was from hearing the past relived, or from the fact that she was trying so hard to humor me. Either way, it didn't matter, for Doctor Rosemary was still determined that laughter *was* the best medicine.

"But, you know, we should have named that bull Mickey since we had so many ball games out in the pasture with him."

"Mickey?" Mama asked, her face in a confused expression.

"Yeah, you know, as in Mantle."

I loved the way her confusion turned into a twisted grin. I knew the next story would get a rise out of her.

"Hey, Mama, speaking of ballgames, do you remember the day that Tina got married, and the whole family all went back to Grandma Miller's house after the wedding?"

Mama had turned her head enough that I could see into her eyes. It was obvious from her expression that she knew what was coming. I continued with delight, excited that I had hit a chord of interest.

"I was so proud. I had on that gorgeous sky blue dress made out of taffeta. It was the first long dress I ever had. And it had that ridiculous big bow on the back of it, but I guess that was the fashion craze back then. Anyway, I thought I was 'the stuff.' I even had those cloth shoes that were dyed to match the dress. And I know Daddy paid a fortune for that get-up, because I can still remember him fussing about how long he had to work to pay for it, much less his tuxedo."

Thinking back to my father's humble beginnings, it dawned on the me that this cousin's wedding was probably the first time Daddy had ever worn a "monkey suit," or "dressed like a penguin," whichever his generation called it. "Was that the first time Daddy ever wore a tuxedo?"

Mama gave a light nod of her head. "He had been in other weddings, but the guys had worn regular suits in those."

"Did he like it?"

"Rosemary, you may have a wonderful father, but he's still a man. He had to carry on for a while about it choking him and all, but that was just for attention. Sure, he liked the way he looked in it. When you got married, he never even made the first grunt."

I snickered. Mama had that male thing pegged to a tee.

"Anyway, do you remember when we got back to Grandma Miller's and all the guys went out to the pasture to play baseball? And when we finished, I came back in the front door."

"All I remember is that horrible smell. You must have stepped in every cow pile in that pasture." Mama had come to life again. Her face had taken on a slight glow, and I could see the twinkle making its way back into her eyes, if only for a brief moment. I would take all I could get.

"No, I had to hold up that long dress and run as hard as I could. I didn't have time to be watching out for where Buttercup had been."

"What were you thinking, playing ball in those formal clothes anyway?"

"I was thinking that I wasn't going to let the boys have all the fun. I had always been a part of every party, and I wasn't going to let some dumb old dress, pretty or not, change that. I had my reputation to look out for!"

"Well, your reputation certainly escalated that day. Every one of your aunts and cousins were howling when you walked through the house with brown spots all around the hem of the dress. You left those heels, stained in brown, by the front door, but the smell still nearly suffocated us!"

"You want to know the only thing I hate about that whole ordeal?" I asked, innocently.

"What's that?"

"That I did not have enough foresight to invent the cow-patty bingo that some of these southern schools use for a fund-raiser." I saw the delight in Mama's face at my humor. "Can you believe that someone from IBM came up with that ridiculous idea?"

"Well, you know what they always say," Mama offered, with her own serious tone. Not expecting her to be as much of a smart-aleck as I was, I was caught off-guard when she added, "Great minds think alike!"

By this point, we were both laughing uncontrollably. Mama was laughing at one of my childhood bloopers, and I was laughing at the fact that my mother was making jokes and enjoying life. It mattered not to me that it was her past life. It was life. We could get to smiles about future life in due time. But, for the moment, it was enough to keep my spirits up until the next time. *And Mama's, too!*, I prayed.

Mama slept most of the way home. I knew that I had worn her completely out with the activities of the day. But I also knew that neither of us would have missed anything that had happened during the course of our journey.

She woke up just as I pulled into my driveway. I had earlier decided, rightly, that she would need to stay at my house overnight and make the trip back up the mountain on the next day. Now I was grateful for my foresight.

Jim met us at the door, and seeing how tired Mama looked, offered to take care of all the things in the car while I got her comfortable for the evening. While she was in the bathroom, I turned down her covers in the guest bedroom, and laid a small pod of red pepper on the pillow.

There was an appreciative smile as she placed the pepper on the dresser, and got into the bed.

"Rosemary?" Her soft voice called me back into the room after I turned out the light.

"Yes?" I returned, expecting her normal two words after such a pleasurable experience.

"It's Pattin' Soul Leather, not Patent Sole Leather."

"Yes, ma'am," I answered, in the same genteel voice that she had used in passing down a bit of her country raising.

My mother was a quiet soul, but she was so full of humor that I saw, during those few words, that her life had been full of laughter. She had her own unique wit that needed no voice. And she had gotten the last word of the day, not to be outdone.

That's my mother! I smiled, closing the door behind me, proud that God had seen fit to allow me to be all those years ago.

Twelve

*T*he weight was falling off Mama so rapidly that you could almost watch it as you looked at her. Even the size-two clothes that she had recently purchased were now hanging loose on her. I could not perceive how anyone could actually hold onto life at her size. Yet, she was hardly any more feeble than I was.

Today began the last round of her treatments. Having lost an entire quarter of her body weight, Mama had made the decision not to take the radiation treatments. Frankly, I was glad for her choice, although I would have never admitted it. Aunt Louise and I were terrified that in her frail condition, it would do more damage than long-term good. Thus, she had been given a two-week break, and we were heading into another six weeks of visits to the oncology center.

It tore at my heart to go into the chemotherapy sessions with her, watching the nurses miss her veins again and again. Nurses rarely hit my veins on the first try, either, but it was different when this was happening to my mother, the person who had given me life.

I finally couldn't bear to watch the nurse stick her anymore. My gut reaction was to scream at the technician to stop. But I knew that would only make everyone more tense, and the nurse hated this as much as I did. Besides, she had already called for reinforcements. I looked up into the face of the newest nurse who had just come in to try her luck at poking my mother.

"Is there anything that she can do to make this problem easier?" I finally asked, out of desperation.

"She is terribly dehydrated. You've absolutely *got* to get more water in her," the new nurse offered.

At this point, I wanted to scream at Mama. She didn't like the thought of drinking water any more than I did, and I knew that her attitude would be like most Southern women who, if they had not done it all these years, they would not start now. Deeper than that, I knew how many nights Mama had spent in the bathroom, for hours on end, and her fear of being like that was worse than the fear of countless sticks by a needle.

Okay, Dr. Rosemary. She heard what the nurse said. She's made it through nearly seventy years of life without your advice, so don't start giving it now. Cheree Miller is fully capable of understanding the consequences from whatever way she decides to go with this. Let it go.

I smiled at my mother, wishing I could take the needles and drink the water for her, and realizing exactly how she had felt with me all those years whenever I had been sick. The same nurturing eyes that were clearly visible on my grandfather's face, Mama's father, in the pictures of him caring for me as an infant, were ones that I had seen many times from her. Now I wondered if she saw those same eyes of concern glaring back at her through me.

It also struck me that I had been right in my assessment that my parents deserved their spacious home overlooking Glassy Mountain, where they could relax and enjoy life for themselves. Like many adults, they had raised their child, and then taken on the responsibility of raising four more children, their own parents. And I was sure that they had not minded any more than I minded being with Mama at the moment. My only regret was that I could not take the pain and hurt for her.

The only thing I could do was offer support during the two-hour ordeal, which generally worked itself into three hours by the time the nurses got Mama's blood pressure under control, and then got the needles into her veins. I didn't think she was strong enough to endure any more of this, but she continued to smile and go on, basking in the joy of all the complications she was not suffering, rather than the few she was.

Therefore, I made it my duty to endure these ordeals with her. And I had come prepared today, bearing entertainment. I reached into my computer case and pulled out the now infamous scrapbook and photo album. Before I had time to open the pages, Mama was already shaking her head, getting her laughter mode in gear.

"Okay, for today's presentation," I began, "we have a Chinese tomato picker."

The picture on the page portrayed a young girl, in a sleeveless shirt, Capri pants, and a pointed, conical, Chinese-looking hat. A small hand was holding a tomato up to the child's mouth, which was already open in anticipation of the delectable taste fresh from the garden.

"Do you remember getting that hat?" Mama asked.

"I sure do. You and Grandma Rose had taken me to downtown Charlotte. We always went there to do our shopping once a week, and then ate lunch at one of the cafeterias. While Grandma Rose was doing her usual number of looking through the pots and pans, I happened to spy that hat. It was one of the few times that I ever remember touching anything without first asking permission, but I grabbed that hat, put it on, and pretended to pull a rickshaw."

"That's right. We didn't have a clue as to how you even knew what a rickshaw was, but you looked so funny, that Mama had to buy that hat, just so you could show Daddy."

"I must have liked it because I see it in several of the pictures."

"You did wear it a lot for a while, especially when you went out in the garden to help. I'm not sure what ever did happen to that hat, but it was good for a few laughs."

"From the looks of these pictures, I should have been called 'The Tomato Bandit.'"

"You did love tomatoes," Mama replied, a story of her own evident in her voice. "I'll never forget one year when the plants weren't doing as well as usual. I had been eyeing a tomato, the first of the season, for several days, waiting for it to ripen so we could have it sliced for dinner with fresh beans and corn. One day, while you were outside playing and I was in the kitchen fixing dinner, I happened to look out the window and notice that the tomato wasn't on the vine. Curious as to what had happened to it, I started toward the back door just in time to see you walk around the corner biting into it."

"Did I get in trouble?" I asked, remembering the fact that I had pulled the tomato off the vine and dug in, but not recalling the after-effects.

"No. The look of satisfaction on your face was worth the wait of another tomato. If someone got that much pleasure out of it, it had served its purpose, as far as I was concerned. Besides, it wasn't long after that when we found out that you were allergic to tomatoes and couldn't have them anymore."

"I got it. God made sure I didn't take anymore of your tomatoes!" I joked.

"Or strawberries, or corn, or green beans, or chocolate! There was a whole list of things you couldn't eat."

"How well I remember. Thank God that I outgrew all those food allergies!" This time I wasn't joking. "But I also remember the day that the doctor said I could eat them again. You made corn and green beans and tomatoes and fresh biscuits. I ate until I was so sick, I was up all night."

"And you didn't want them for a long time after that, again."

I chuckled, remembering that episode a little more than I wished at the moment. "I guess God knew better than the doctors, huh?"

My mother and I looked at each other, neither of us speaking, but both thinking about the words I had just said. This seemed like another of those times. We quietly looked through the pictures for the rest of the time at the oncology center, until the nurse came in and announced that Mama had only a few more minutes left for the day.

That does it! I can't let this day end on such a solemn note.

I grabbed the photo album from my mother and quickly turned the pages, looking for a loose-leaf sheet I had stuck inside the back cover.

"And for the day's grand finale," I announced, in the manner of the ringmaster at the circus, "we have a poem by my Uncle Edwin, written when he was only a young lad."

Mama glared at me. "You are not going to read that out loud in here," she said, in a reprimanding voice that sensed it was speaking wasted words.

"I most certainly am. I happen to be very proud of the fact that I come from such an artistic family!"

I was aware that the poem might cause her lady-like face to blush, but it was one of those fond remembrances from her childhood. They had lived off the main highway, and the dirt road by their house was in horrible condition. The county was supposed to be putting gravel on it, and the highway commission was scheduled to take a look at it on that day.

When Grandpa went to work that morning, there was a huge painted sign at the corner of the main highway and the road to his house. Uncle Edwin had the foresight to also write the poem in the front of the family's dictionary, in ink, for all posterity, knowing that Grandma Rose would get rid of the sign the minute she saw it, but she would not throw away something so valuable to her children's education. Thus, the poem, which was now cherished by my children, as well, would likely make it into eternity.

I leaned forward and with great aplomb read,
> *This road is not passable,*
> *not even jack-ass-able,*

> *If you want to travel it,*
> *get out and gravel it!*

Amidst the laughter from Mama and Daddy and her nurse, I asked, "So, did it work?"

"What?" my mother asked, wiping the tears with her free hand, struggling to hear me through all the commotion I had caused.

"The poem. Did it work?"

"Yes, it worked. The state trucks came out and graveled the road a couple of days later."

We were laughing so hard at this point that the rest of the nurses had to come and see what they had missed. That only fueled the flame, so I had to tell the story and read the poem all over again, causing Mama to blush even more, all the while laughing, and wiping the tears.

I put the book away so that the nurse could run the saline solution through Mama's veins, cleaning them out and getting her ready to go home to face another week of further dehydration. This was the last time I would come with her until the last treatment, and I hoped that the day's activities would make the next few weeks easier. I would leave Daddy a note to pack the photo album each week before they came here, hoping it would provide more than the empty words of the magazines.

Thirteen

I retreated to the screened porch when we got home from the last chemotherapy treatment. What a rejoicing we had had. Mama, looking terribly worn and frail, had jumped up and down when the nurse removed the needles from her arm for the very last time. Her face showed nothing but the exhilaration of a young child anticipating a special occasion. The spirited light of her faith shone all around her.

She truly IS a light. A light unto the world. A shining light in my world and for all those who know her, I thought as we exited the building.

The nurses and the other patients looked on Mama with admiration – smiling, laughing, enjoying the moment with her. I couldn't help but think about the Boardwalk in San Diego, and the warm afternoon we had jumped over the posts and skipped down the sidewalk.

When we walked outside, the ominous clouds of the morning had given way to a mist of cold, chilling rain. I quickly unlocked the car, not wanting Mama to get chilled. But her excitement of the moment seemed to ward off all the other dangers that threatened to penetrate her body during its weakness.

I had known that my mother would do something to remember when she got out of that chaise for the last time. Cheree Miller was a fighter. She was small. She was quiet. But she was a warrior. God's warrior. She had a statement to make. Just as her deeds had made a statement her entire life.

My heart filled to overflowing with pride as I reflected over not just the day, but the past several months. It was only five more days until a new year would begin, so it was easy to allow my mind to wander down a lane filled with memories of what had been, of what had not been, and of what was to come.

Mama was supposed to have had two more weeks of treatment, but she wanted so badly to be done with it, that Dr. Fisher finally made the decision to let her go. I think he saw that her positive attitude, strong beliefs, and family support were truly more healing than anything they could run through the IV tubes.

Thus it was that she finished her treatments today, on the exact date that had originally been calculated. She was ecstatic in that fact alone, knowing that she truly could put this episode behind her and begin a new year, cancer-free and back to her normal routine of no medicine.

We all knew that the surgeon was going to keep close tabs on her, requiring exams every six months, rather than annually. And we knew that those exams would be at the hospital, with her being put to sleep, rather than with local anesthesia. But Dr. Stallings had agreed that the God-forsaken "go juice," as we all called it, was going to be traded for something that Mama's system could handle a little easier, so she was gaining ground.

And we all knew that Dr. Fisher was going to see Mama every two months to check her blood, and make sure that her body was doing its own part to keep up its defenses from the terrorist that had tried to lay claim on her life. With the pleasant relationship between his patients and his nurses and staff, that was going to seem like a fun visit rather than a medical necessity, so that would be easily tolerable.

Mama was in the bathroom, the last of her treatments taking its toll on her. She was prepared for the weeks of lingering after-effects, knowing that she had made it through the battle. She had come out a victor, and as she had proudly proclaimed as she walked out the door - to the nurses, to Daddy and me, to all who would listen, but mostly to herself - "I don't have cancer anymore."

My attention turned to my surroundings. I would have to leave this place in a few minutes to head back down the mountain to a life of my own. As I stood there, gazing and thinking, I could hear the voice of silence – the one that I knew Mama had heard countless times. *I'd stay in the garden with him though the night around me be falling, but he bids me go, thru the voice of woe his voice to me is calling.* That voice, so clear and sweet. The lush melody, blending with all the sounds of nature. How I longed to stay, to linger, to watch, to listen, to pray . . . but I knew there was Another here to take care of Mama.

There were no flowers visible on the ground below me. But I knew that within only a couple of months, Mama's light, and the Source that gave her that light, would have radiated until all the bulbs in the ground, and all the plants hidden in the cold earth would soon be making their way to appear and bloom in all their fullness.

Mama would once again be able to sit in the warmth of the sun in her rocker on the screened porch – her mansion on the hilltop. And before too much longer she would be able to venture out into the yard, where she could walk and talk with the One who had given her this life . . and she would be able to tarry . . . all day long . . . . *in the garden.*

IN THE GARDEN

I come to the garden alone
while the dew is still on the roses,
And the voice I hear falling on my ear,
the Son of God discloses.
And he walks with me, and he talks with me,
and he tells me I am his own;
And the joy we share as we tarry there,
none other has ever known.

He speaks, and the sound of his voice
is so sweet the birds hush their singing,
And the melody that he gave to me
within my heart is ringing.
And he walks with me, and he talks with me,
and he tells me I am his own;
And the joy we share as we tarry there,
none other has ever known.

I'd stay in the garden with him
though the night around me be falling,
But he bids me go; thru the voice of woe
his voice to me is calling.
And he walks with me, and he talks with me,
and he tells me I am his own;
And the joy we share as we tarry there,
none other has ever known.

- - C. Austin Miles

Love Lifted Me
(*First volume of Eagle's Wings Trilogy*)

Now Available

Catherine Ritch Guess

Christina Cache, a well-educated and well-traveled minister, is literally 'thrown' into the face (and arms) of Shane Sievers, a "bad boy" who has just attempted suicide while strung out on cocaine, and who has spent his entire adolescent and adult life in places that she has spent hers trying to avoid. This twice-divorced mother of two miraculously finds out that this is the most witty, intelligent, compassionate man she has ever met.

The struggle emerges as Christina, with her wholesome and angelic qualities, battles the evil of Shane's uttermost worldly existence, and the depths of his earthly hell created by his now thoroughly outcast position in society.

Their five-month journey down the same path teaches them of a love far greater than any physical or emotional sense of the word, and each emerges as a totally different entity who has reached a completeness never before known.

Higher Ground

(*Second volume of Eagle's Wings Trilogy*)

Coming for Summer, 2002

Catherine Ritch Guess

Because of a recent and strange friendship with the most unlikely of soul mates, Christina Cache dares to take the necessary leap to follow her calling. Ever willing and anxious to face a challenge, she leaves her comfort zone, finding herself with a new home *and* a new career.

Equipped with little more than her intellect, her talent, and life's brutal lessons, the determined survivor sets out to conquer this seemingly insurmountable goal. Hard work, faith, and perseverance pay off as she climbs the peak in search of her new life.

But, in having to virtually start from ground zero, Christina finds that the greatest reward of finally topping her summit is in helping others reach their own higher ground.

In the Bleak Midwinter

Coming for Christmas 2002

Catherine Ritch Guess

To Celia, it was simply the yearly Christmas concert at the private school. Of course, it *was* the first year in their new facility, and the local media was to be on hand, so in a sense, just maybe it *was* going to be a special evening. But to the burned-out music teacher, it still seemed no more than another night of getting dressed in her finest, only to watch seven-hundred children do the same.

However, as her elite boys' choir sang *Gesu Bambino*, their pure voices perfectly on pitch and their Latin enunciation impeccable, Celia was overcome by the sound of a baby's low cry. Feeling "strangely warmed", in the words of John Wesley, she dismissed it as an emotional moment caused by the glow of lights, and the glitz of the regal, deep-purple velvet stage curtain.

Little did she know that, before the night was over, she was going to discover the most memorable gift of her life, and give her beloved students the most valuable lesson they would ever learn.

2003 Releases

- - - - - - -

On Eagle's Wings
(Third volume of Eagle's Wings Trilogy)
Coming for Spring, 2003

Peace in the Valley
Coming for Summer, 2003

Wind Beneath My Wings
(Postlude to Eagle's Wings Trilogy)
Coming for Fall, 2003

ADVANCE ORDER FORM

Book Title _____

Name _____

Address _____

Phone number _____

e-mail address _____

(Send to)
CRM
P.O. Box 367, Paw Creek, NC 28130
1-866-CRM-BOOK
FAX – 704-391-1698
www.ciridmus.com

ADVANCE ORDER FORM

Book Title _____

Name _____

Address _____

Phone number _____

e-mail address _____

(Send to)
CRM
P.O. Box 367, Paw Creek, NC 28130
1-866-CRM-BOOK
FAX – 704-391-1698
www.ciridmus.com

The Ritch Guess Collection

Beginning with the release of **Higher Ground** in the summer of 2002, there will be a collection of puzzles, note cards, and prints of the covers for all the future books by Catherine Ritch Guess.

CRM has contracted with two North Carolina artists, Ruth Ellen Busbee and Prudy Weaver, to do paintings for all future covers of books by Guess.

Prudy Weaver, a watercolor artist, is painting all the cover artwork for the *Eagle's Wings Trilogy*. Ruth Ellen Busbee, an acrylic artist, will have one of her paintings featured on the cover of *In the Bleak Midwinter*.

Both of these women will be appearing with Guess at book premieres, signings, and art shows in the near future. Dates for their appearances will appear on the CRM website in the late summer.

Please contact CRM if you would like more information, or to schedule a public appearance in your area.

About the Author

Catherine Ritch Guess, also a published composer, is currently working on a recording to go with each of her book titles. When she is not making music at Pleasant Grove UMC in Charlotte, NC, where she is the Minister of Music, she can be found either in the Blue Ridge Mountains of North Carolina, or the deserts of Arizona, writing another novel.

Guess, who holds degrees in Church Music, Music Ed and a Master's Degree in Christian Education, is a Diaconal Minister of the United Methodist Church.